PURSUIT

PURSUIT

THE BALVENIE STORIES
COLLECTION

—

Edited by Alex Preston

CANONGATE

First published in Great Britain, the USA and Canada in 2019
by Canongate Books Ltd, 14 High Street, Edinburgh EH1 1TE

Distributed in the USA by Publishers Group West
and in Canada by Publishers Group Canada

canongate.co.uk

1

British Library Cataloguing-in-Publication Data
A catalogue record for this book is available on
request from the British Library

ISBN 978 1 78689 901 9

Edited by Alex Preston
Designed by Here Design

Typeset in Plantin MT Pro by
Palimpsest Book Production Ltd, Falkirk, Stirlingshire

Printed and bound in Great Britain by Clays Ltd, Elcograf S.p.A.

CONTENTS

—

PREFACE

Gemma Louise Paterson,
The Balvenie Global Ambassador

I TELL stories about whisky for a living. When I take people round The Balvenie Distillery, they'll hear, in several chapters, how barley becomes malt whisky. They'll meet an array of fascinating characters – the crafts-people who work here making casks, turning grain, firing the malt kiln, watching the stills and mending the copper, or tilling the earth and then sowing more barley. But it's the final part of the whisky-making story that contains the most suspense – as we put the liquid into barrels and hand it back to nature, sometimes for decades. This is when the more complex flavours are created, as spirit and oak enter a dialogue. Minor characters play important roles here, too: the traces of sherry or bourbon each cask once held; the quirks that make every one different. Each cask is as unique as a snowflake, a fingerprint: the provenance of the tree, the porosity of the oak, and the craftsmanship of the cooper. As all these stories play out, they are shaped by The Balvenie malt master, David Stewart MBE, and his apprentice malt master, Kelsey McKechnie, who sample and nose the evolving liquids and select which casks to bottle and which to nurture longer. David and Kelsey are our editors, deciding which stories have found their happy ending and which must be kept for a later volume.

The other whisky stories I tell are when I conduct a tasting. Each whisky has a unique flavour profile – its balance of sweet and honey over oak, delicate fruits and citrus over minerality, for example – and tell how each element makes itself known in every single sip. A whisky carries within it the story of its origins, a unique memoir involving, among other factors, what kind of casks it was matured in, where the barley came from, and was it peated to add a wisp of smoke? These sub-plots inspired a new range, The Balvenie Stories, whiskies that represent slight twists in the tale, the results of experiments such as toasting the barrel, or adding extra peat sourced from the Highlands to the kiln, or perhaps a sprig of heather. These fresh narratives are how we keep the whisky-making story evolving, how we pursue greatness in our craft.

This idea of stories written in whisky inspired us to make a book. And chasing an ideal became its theme: determination, perseverance, resolve – *Pursuit*. What a book it has turned out to be! We're proud so many great writers have contributed, and are inspired by the quality and range of the stories they've written.

Finally, I'll say that we always imagined these stories as the perfect accompaniment to a dram or two of The Balvenie, so I'll raise a toast to everyone involved in creating the book you're holding and hand over to Alex to introduce the stories you're about to enjoy. *Slàinte!*

INTRODUCTION
Alex Preston

WE read stories, the American novelist John Barth tells us, not principally to find out what happens next, but rather to answer 'the essential question of identity – the personal, professional, cultural, even species-specific "Who Am I?"' Stories help us to define ourselves, to record and interrogate our actions and motives, to understand backwards a life lived forwards. Our lives are shaped by stories, by the need to fashion frantic, random existence into something linear and comprehendible. Our quest for meaning in our lives is actually just the search for a story we can really believe in. There is something compulsive, even desperate, in our need to tell and to hear, to be heard. We are the stories we tell about ourselves.

Stories give us something to strive for. Whether it's the quantum physicist pursuing unified field theory, the master distiller perfecting her blend, or the free diver seeking to plumb the lonely depths of the oceans, the grandest feats of human achievement – the acts of genius, inspiration and gritty endeavour that push our species forward – all take place within the context of stories. Our most brilliant and heroic accomplishments form part of a greater collective narrative: a universal story about individual application and sacrifice leading to societal benefit, a tale of odds overcome, dreams pursued, fears mastered, of breakthroughs and epiphanies and moments of sublime triumph.

Last year, just as I was beginning to think about putting this collection together, I was invited to Turkey to swim the Hellespont. This notorious stretch of water, which divides Europe and Asia, is not only one of the world's busiest shipping lanes; it also has currents of extraordinary ferocity, sitting as it does just where the Black Sea, through the neck of the Bosphorus, disgorges itself into the Aegean. The Hellespont has a long history in literature and legend. Ovid told of Leander, who was drowned swimming to visit his lover, Hero. The poet Byron made two attempts to traverse it, turning back once, then completing the crossing in May 1810. After his success, he wrote to his mother, 'I plume myself on this achievement more than I could possibly do on any kind of glory, poetical, political or rhetorical.'

I'd never been much of a swimmer as a kid, but then in my teens I read a book that changed my life – Charles Sprawson's *Haunts of the Black Masseur*, a paean to the mystical allure of swimming, a history of extraordinary acts of endurance and endeavour by swimmers fabled and forgotten. I loved the book so much that I wrote to Sprawson, and we began a correspondence. I also started to swim. A few years ago, I heard from a mutual friend that Charles, who was in his early seventies, had had a fall. I went to visit him in hospital in west London, where I found him in a terrible state. He'd been battered by a series of illnesses, and had just been diagnosed with the initial stages of vascular dementia. He was largely coherent, but gave the sense of someone who'd been caught by surprise by the dark twist his life had taken.

Charles swam the Hellespont with his daughter in the early 1990s; I undertook my own crossing more than a quarter of a century later in honour of him. As I set off into the turbid, fast-flowing waters last summer, I thought of Charles, who'd been moved from the hospital to a nursing home, and who would likely never see his beloved Mediterranean again. The swim itself was gruelling, occasionally horrifying, ultimately magnificent. I was followed by a flotilla of support boats, while over to my right, past the jaws of the Dardanelles, vast tankers idled as they waited for me to cross. Beyond these floating cities, towards Greece, I could just make out the ancient site of Troy. Nearer were the beaches of Gallipoli, where so many had been brave, so many died. This was a landscape dense with history. What kept me going over the seven kilometres I swam that day, the first three against a current of powerful and insidious intensity, were stories. The story of a great writer laid low by fate, the story of the authors and heroes who'd made the swim before, the proximity of tragedy, the possibility of failure, the thrill of success. As I came into the harbour of Çanakkale, just over an hour after I'd set out, there were TV crews and newspaper reporters, a small but gratifyingly enthusiastic crowd. The surge of joy I felt on completing the swim caught me by surprise. I recognised the addictive tug it asserted on me.

That evening, contemplating my return home, I remembered something that Charles had said to me before I set out. Whatever his life had in store for him, he'd mused, no one would ever be able to take away the fact that he had conquered the Hellespont. It was one of the central chapters in the story of his life, as it was to become one of mine. In writing of it, I add my voice to all those other voices – Charles's included – who have told of the depths and the currents, the jellyfish and sharks, the fear and its mastery. It is one of the stories that makes me who I am, part of the infinite and glorious tapestry of stories that tells us who we are as a species. And this is what the collection you're about to read is all about: a celebration of endeavour that is itself a work of noble endeavour. Our literature remains one of our grandest achievements and there are some extraordinary contributions here.

I'm enormously proud of all of the stories in this collection, which have taken the brief – tales of human endeavour with a twist – and interpreted them in such vivid, different and powerfully affecting ways. The stories range wildly across time and space, lacing between fact and fiction, from the epic to the intimate. They share an essential truth, though: a well-lived life is about perseverance, single-mindedness and the dogged pursuit of the things we care about, notwithstanding the possibility of failure.

These are stories from a host of the most exciting voices in contemporary literature, which will entertain, inspire and challenge. Some, like Kamila Shamsie's voyage to Antarctica in the footsteps of Shackleton or Peter Frankopan's tale of life in the gulag, tell us about the dangerous edges of human experience. Others, like Tash Aw's story about a young boy's relationship with his father, or Max Porter's tale of the daily grind, are about a different kind of endeavour, a different breed of courage. All of the stories here will leave you knowing more about the human condition, about the pain of failure and the joy of success, about why we sacrifice the best parts of our lives in pursuit of our dreams.

TIME AND TIME AGAIN
Eley Williams

> How well the skilful gard'ner drew
> Of flow'rs and herbs this dial new;
> Where from above the milder sun
> Does through a fragrant zodiac run;
> And, as it works, th' industrious bee
> Computes its time as well as we.
> How could such sweet and wholesome hours
> Be reckon'd but with herbs and flow'rs!
>
> — FROM ANDREW MARVELL'S *THE GARDEN*

I RECOGNISED him from the care home. The nurse's name was Amir and he blinked in the beam of my torch. I tried to keep my adrenaline in check and held my voice low. When I spoke I sounded more surprised than angry. 'What are you doing?'

He swept a thumb across his forehead. It left a faint trail of mud above his eye. Maybe it was manure, compost, topsoil. Honestly, I've no idea what the difference is. Not a green finger in my body, or whatever the phrase is.

'I'm gardening,' said Amir. Somewhere in the trees beyond the fence in the darkness an owl hooted and we both jumped.

'It's three o'clock in the morning.' I cast my torch about. Trowels, little pots and bulbs, a watering can.

'Yes,' he said, glancing at his feet. 'I thought it must be.'

'*Gardening?*' I repeated. Amir didn't say anything so I went on: 'I just happened to be watching the CCTV and you popped up.' I tried to maintain an even tone. 'I thought you were breaking in.'

1

I could see Amir was abashed. He did not put down his tools, however. 'This is the first time you've noticed in three years,' he said.

'Three years?' He twiddled with his spade handle as I spluttered. 'You're lucky I didn't come out with the dog!' I stood a little straighter and tried to muster an air of authority. I had to raise my voice over the owl. 'We could have woken residents and you'd be hauled before management. Did you say you've been doing this for *three years*? After work, between shifts? You've been coming here?'

Amir was still in his work trousers, the same dark blue uniform that all nurses and members of staff wear at the care home. I'm the only one who gets a black uniform with the word SECURITY stitched over the breast-pocket.

'Please,' Amir said. 'It's only gardening. Please don't tell. It's a favour to someone.'

I looked around the plot. I never really came out to this part of the grounds. There were neat little beds planted in careful rows.

'It's only gardening,' Amir said again. 'I can – look, can I meet you tomorrow and maybe explain?'

'Surely they have contractors,' I said. 'Ground staff . . . this feels like trespassing.' I coughed. 'It *is* trespassing.'

'This is special work,' said Amir. He stepped carefully around the plant-bed. 'Please. I can explain tomorrow.'

I tried to seem steely. I had heard about Amir. He was highly regarded amongst the care home staff. I put what I hoped was a kindly hand on his shoulder and I could feel the damp of sweat through his shirt. He must have been at work out here for hours.

'Meet me tomorrow?' he asked again. I kept my torch on his face and he did not drop his gaze.

✣

We met in my office, Amir bouncing in through the door looking fresh as a daisy. This was disarming: I had thought he might be contrite or about to tell me that he had handed in his notice.

'Have you met Mr Waverley?' Amir asked by way of greeting.

'Is he on the staff?' The name did ring a bell. I collected myself and gestured at my CCTV monitor. 'Amir. What were you playing at last night?'

'He's a resident,' Amir said. 'Mr Waverley. I want you to see him.' He literally tugged at my sleeve.

I said, 'Wait a minute. I don't want to get you in trouble and we all have different ways of dealing with stress, but I can't have you up at all hours doing secret "gardening". It's not right. I could lose my job and you certainly could. I really should be taking this issue higher up.'

'Don't say it like that,' Amir said, miming the air-quotes that I had carved through the air with my fingers. 'It *is* gardening.'

'Whatever.' I put unconvinced fervour on the word. 'Amir, I can't turn a blind eye.'

'I was replanting the pimpernels,' Amir said.

I stared at him.

'They prefer soils in the pH range 5.5 to 8.0,' he clarified.

'I really don't care,' I said.

Amir looked hurt. 'Will you come meet him? Mr Waverley?'

I pretended to check my schedule.

❖

Mr Waverley was sitting in one of the comfier chairs in the care home's conservatory. I recognised him vaguely from the corridors and from communal meal times: a soft-spoken, polite gentleman with a thick white head of hair and a strong jaw. As we approached, Amir gave him a little wave. I said my hellos and Mr Waverley fished a hand into his wallet. I'm used to this. A lot of the residents like to show me pictures of their family or loved ones in well-thumbed photographs.

'This is me in Belize.' Mr Waverley proffered the photograph. It showed a handsome man wearing a stained shirt and khaki shorts. He must have been in his thirties. The photo showed him squatting in a shallow riverbank, grinning. I handed the picture back.

'Did you see what's in his hand there?' Amir asked. I squinted.

'*Dactylorhiza waverlii*,' Mr Waverley intoned. He seemed to relish every syllable. 'Nice little orange one there.'

'He has an orchid named after him!' Amir said. He hovered by Mr Waverley's elbow, a look of excitement on his face. 'He discovered it and they named it after him! Can you imagine?'

'That's great,' I said. It was. I wished I had looked more carefully at the photograph but Mr Waverley had folded it back up and repocketed it.

'Cormac, isn't it?' Mr Waverley said to me. This took me aback. No one usually bothers to ask Security's name.

'That's right,' I said and tapped my ID badge.

'Some people think that name means *son of the charioteer*,' Mr Waverley said.

'Sounds good to me,' I said.

Mr Waverley went on, 'Others think it means *son of defilement*.' Amir suppressed a laugh.

'Less good,' I said.

'Mr Waverley told me that my name means either *prince* or *sunlit portion of a tree*,' said the nurse. He had a huge grin on his face.

'*Topmost boughs*,' said Mr Waverley.

'Is that right?' I said. 'A little inexact, all this,' I observed.

'And,' said Mr Waverley, warming to his subject and overlooking my interjection, 'my surname comes from an old English word meaning *meadow of quivering aspens*.'

These pleasantries were all very well but I wanted to nip this situation in the bud. 'I'm here because I came across Amir's little early morning hobby,' I said.

Mr Waverley and Amir shared a look.

'Amir is doing it all under my instruction,' Mr Waverley said after a while, clearing his throat. 'He hasn't taken a penny for it either.'

'I wouldn't dream of it!' said Amir. 'It's a pleasure. Pure pleasure.'

'And I would be out there myself if it wasn't for the state of my back and the arthritis,' said Mr Waverley. He glared at his hands.

'Mr Waverley and I have been talking for years about gardens and plants,' said Amir. He drew a chair up to the older man so that they could sit closer together. They unconsciously angled their shoulders towards one another. 'He can tell you about every plant-derived drug in the book.'

'Not just plants. Of the most-prescribed 150 prescription drugs,' Mr Waverley said, 'at least 118 are based on natural sources, did you know? At least 3 per cent come from vertebrate species such as snakes or frogs.' This was the most animated I'd ever seen him. Usually he was a taciturn man. Polite, as I say, but not exactly a chatterbox.

Amir was enthralled. 'Are you getting this, Cormac? The *recall* that this man has!'

'That's great,' I said. 'But I'm here to talk about the gardening.'

The two men moved their heads closer together and set their lips in a firm line. I crossed my arms.

'You look like a pair of conspirators. What's going on?'

'I can explain,' said Mr Waverley. Nobody spoke.

'Are you growing drugs?' I said finally. Some of the

other residents in the conservatory glanced our way then returned to their chess games and coffee.

Both men, nurse and resident, looked appalled.

'Good Lord, no!' said Mr Waverley. 'Amir here,' and the older man placed a hand upon the younger man's shoulder, 'is helping me build a clock.'

I thought I must have misheard.

'A clock,' I repeated.

'Yes! Carl Linnaeus first thought of it. He called it *Horologium Florae*. Of course,' Mr Waverley said, clearly warming to his subject, 'Linnaeus's flowering times are based on the climate and sunshine hours of eighteenth-century Uppsala, where he taught, so we're having to adapt a fair bit for a south-facing garden in Maidenhead.'

'Mr Waverley had me order all these books about Linnaeus to the library,' Amir said. 'I've got a whole bookshelf dedicated to him in the break room.'

'It's great to have a student again,' Mr Waverley said. 'I used to work and lecture at Kew Gardens, you know.'

I spread my hands, trying to stem the flow of their conversation.

'This is all fascinating,' I said, 'and I care, I really do, but I need to know you're not doing anything untoward late at night on the care home's grounds. And I need you both to reassure me that it won't happen again. It's a question of health and safety.'

'You've heard of Linnaeus, I presume?' Mr Waverley asked. He looked over his glasses at me.

'That's neither here nor there,' I attempted to say.

'He dedicated his life to creating a classification system of plants, animals,' said Amir.

Mr Waverley nodded. 'All living organisms.'

'You know when an animal or plant has a Latin name in italics?' said Amir. '*Felis catus* for domestic cats, that kind of thing. That's thanks to Linnaeus.'

'Rousseau called him "the greatest man on earth",' Mr Waverley chipped in. 'And Goethe called him a genius on the same scale as Shakespeare.' The older man closed his eyes, and a smile made his face glow. Years seemed to fall off him just by thinking about this topic. 'Imagine being remembered like that.'

'You two are big fans, I get it,' I said. 'But, please. The matter in hand.'

'It's all relevant,' urged Amir.

'Haven't you got work to be at?' I said, somewhat sharply.

'This is all about healing,' Amir said. We regarded one another for a moment. The sound of the care home air-conditioner buzzed and the chink of china teacups across the room sounded like tiny cathedral bells.

'You mentioned a clock?' I said.

Mr Waverley coughed. 'That I can explain. Something else that Linnaeus hypothesised was that flowers could accurately predict time based on when their blooms opened and when they closed. I mean, lots of people before Linnaeus had observed that some plants raise their leaves during the day then they droop down during the night. Androsthenes did in the time of Alexander the Great, and Pliny the Elder, of course, in the first century.'

'Right, right,' I said, letting the words wash over me.

'But,' said Mr Waverley, sitting up, 'Linnaeus was the first to posit that a garden could be grown so that as the hours change different flowers would be shown to open their blooms. Stick all those flowers in the ground, look after them right and according to when their petals open you can tell the hour of day just by looking out of the window.'

Amir and Mr Waverley shone upon me. Their eyes were wide and gleaming.

'That's nuts,' I said.

Amir pulled a list from somewhere in his uniform. 'You

know the scarlet pimpernel, the thing you saw me laying down this morning?'

'*Anagallis arvensis*,' said Mr Waverley. Amir nodded.

'That opens its flowers at eight a.m. pretty much on the dot. While spotted cat's ear opens at six a.m. and closes between four and five p.m.'

'Excuse me,' I interrupted. '*Spotted cat's ear?*'

'Perennial herb with pale yellow flowers,' Mr Waverley said impatiently. '*Hypochaeris maculata.*'

'It looks a bit like a dandelion,' nodded Amir, trying to be helpful.

'Dandelions open at five a.m. and close at about eight to nine a.m.,' responded Mr Waverley.

'There is no way it can be that exact,' I said. I had decided I should humour them for a bit. Their interest was infectious and it was impressive to hear Mr Waverley call up so much information. This was definitely the longest I've ever heard him speak the whole time he had been in the care home. 'It must be far too haphazard to be of use.'

Mr Waverley snorted dismissively. 'Precision is over-rated,' he said. 'It's the *scope* of vision that's the key. There's never been a successful Linnaean clock. Can you imagine if we pull it off?' And I saw it again: his eyes had a new lustre to them. 'Time rooted right there in the garden, slow and steady in the sunshine?'

'What opens at seven a.m.?' I asked. Mr Waverley rolled his eyes.

'Loads,' volunteered Amir, counting off his fingers. 'I've planted hawkweed, garden lettuce, St Bernard's lily . . .'

'Fine.'

'I introduced bindweed to the car park – it opens reliably at five a.m.,' Amir went on, 'but the council quickly pulled it out because it grows so quickly and was covering the Pay and Display signs.' Mr Waverley reached out and patted Amir's hand.

'But what about, like, three p.m.? Teatime?' I asked.

'That's when marigolds close their flowers,' said Mr Waverley. 'And in late spring the Icelandic poppy closes at seven p.m.'

'You have an answer for everything,' I said.

'A lot of trial and error,' Mr Waverley said. 'A lifetime of it.'

'How much is this all costing you?' I pressed.

Mr Waverley blushed and looked out of the window.

'One can't put a price on achieving your dreams.' Amir took the reins of the conversation. 'Less so,' he went on, 'the dreams of others.'

'I see,' I said.

'It's my pleasure to fund it,' Amir said. He was shrugging. 'Gets me out and about. Soil under your fingernails, watching things grow. It's such a small thing but I haven't felt this well in years.'

'It gives me something to look forward to,' Mr Waverley said in a small voice. 'So much of life is to do with watching and waiting. But cultivating – ah, that's what it's all about.'

'He doesn't get many visitors,' Amir said quietly to me. 'Before he came here, he'd spent his retirement experimenting, seeding, plotting out designs. He's explained it all to me – the need for shade and what needs watering at what stage. It's *extraordinary*, Cormac. He'd almost finished planting a full clock in his back garden before he came here but – well, the landlord dug it all up when he had to leave the building . . .'

Mr Waverley slumped a little in his seat. A cloud moved across the sun and heads of flowers stirred beyond the conservatory window.

'Look,' I said again. 'I can see it means a lot to you. But I can't—'

'He's been tending to the study of living things all his life,' Amir said.

9

I looked at Amir in his dark blue nurse's scrubs. 'Like you,' I said.

'One man's weed is another person's wildflower,' Mr Waverley said. He was looking out at the garden. 'And a wildflower is another person's way of passing the time they have left.'

'It's not hurting anyone,' Amir said.

'We've almost planted the full design,' Mr Waverley said.

We all turned our heads again to look out of the conservatory window. I did not know the names of any of the flowers or bushes there and did not think that I had paid them a second's attention the whole time that I'd worked at the home. I really hadn't registered that a garden was even there. Amir and Mr Waverley were also watching the world beyond the window. No; they were peering at the garden, then the cheap white clock above the Formica coffee table and then looking back to a specific spot in the garden. There were tears of satisfaction in both their eyes.

✛

Mr Waverley suffered a fall later that year and was immobile for the rest of the summer. I brought in a picture frame for his orchid photograph and put it on his dressing-table, and I helped Amir reposition his bed so that Mr Waverley could see out of the window when propped up on pillows.

'Uppsadaisy,' said Amir as he fluffed Mr Waverley's coverlet a little.

'Thank you, treetop,' Mr Waverley said softly. 'And thank you, Cormac,' he said to me. His eye drifted to the window. 'Half-past hawkweed?' he said.

'Round about that,' Amir said, checking his watch.

'We put in some *Mirabilis jalapa* last night,' I added. 'Should come up a treat.'

There were new birds in the garden, and there were

bees and sweet new scents on the breeze. Residents would come and coo as they took turns around the grounds, not knowing they were passing a book of hours, but swapping anecdotes and tips for improving the soil and when to put down netting. And I took my time to stroll there, too, making a point of it every day. I took moments every day to smell the flowers and touch the outermost petals of time embedded and in full bloom.

WEST LAKE
David Szalay

I'M woken by the phone. What time is it? The light around
the curtains seems so weak it could be streetlight at night.
Or could it? No. It has a bluish solidity that manages to
reveal the basic shapes of the room. It must be morning. Then
I pick up on the sound of the rain. It was raining last night
and by the sound it still is, and just as heavily. The sound
comes into the room as a continuous background whisper, like
the whisper from the air-conditioner but wetter. The air-
conditioner is set to heat though it doesn't make the room very
warm except directly underneath it. The phone is still going.
Leaning on my elbow now, noticing (the next thing) the slight,
imprecisely located pain in my head, I answer it. 'Hello?'

'Hello?' I say again.

And then again, 'Hello?'

I put the phone down.

The sound of the rain has somehow acquired more
definition in the last minute, as if it has come into focus.

After a period of lying on my back, staring at the ceiling,
studying the way that the light spreads across it in an infinitely
fine progression from bluish bright just above the drawn
curtains, where the texture of the surface is visible, to more
or less dark at the far wall, where it isn't, I lean over and
look at the time on my own phone.

It is twenty past ten in the morning, apparently.

In England it is twenty past two in the morning. The middle of the night. Most of the people I know are asleep, and will be for hours. It is an odd, lonely feeling. And the other thing is, Western social media doesn't work here. I try Twitter, and then WhatsApp, and nothing happens. That is an odd, lonely feeling too. I spend some minutes thinking about this. Then I put down my phone and walk naked to the bathroom. The bathroom smells of cigarette smoke. The smell is so strong it's as if someone was in there, smoking, during the night. I almost expect to find a butt floating in the toilet bowl. I don't of course. The smell must be coming through the ventilation system, and standing there I peer at the vents while the water in the bowl turns frothily golden.

✦

An hour later, when I leave the hotel, it is still raining. It has been raining like this since I arrived here. With my meagre headache, which is also still going on, I walk along the canal, taking care to avoid puddles. The hotel backs onto a canal-side walk. There's a screen of trees and other plants, quite nicely landscaped, and then the leaden water of the canal. Some of the buildings along this quiet walk are mock-ups of traditional wooden houses – prosperous merchants' houses, they look like – and hidden among the trees there are speakers playing the music of traditional stringed instruments, music that proceeds one drawn-out note at a time.

This all ends in a wooden gate, beyond which lies a major intersection. Sudden twenty-first-century city, with buildings eating into the sky. I wait at the lights, under my umbrella. Diagonally across the intersection is the shopping mall, and the restaurant is in there somewhere. I already know the shopping mall. I was there yesterday. It's very new. Inside, they're still putting up some of the signage and not all of the units are occupied yet. I'm slightly early – I over-estimated how long it would take to walk from the hotel – so I step into Massimo Dutti and look around for a few minutes. I fondle sweater sleeves and look idly at a leather bag. I still feel a bit weird. Leaving Massimo Dutti I have a moment when I don't know where I am. I mean where on planet Earth. I momentarily forget, or lose my hold on the infor-mation. Then I know again. Though even then the knowledge feels disconcertingly abstract.

Escalators slant up through the tall open space at the centre of the mall. The restaurants are all on one of the upper floors, and I ride up past a vast red fibreglass giraffe.

I know Wei. The others I haven't met before. Wei makes the introductions as I take my seat, though I only retain one of the names – Yaya. It's easy to remember and also, I suppose, because the young woman in question is sort of good-looking. She seems American when she talks. She does most of the talking. Sometimes Wei says something. The stress of being the host is visible in his eyes and his posture. It's not a role that comes entirely naturally to him.

When there's a pause, the man sitting on my left, who has shoulder-length grey hair and a long face that looks somehow un-Chinese, says to me, 'You're a writer?'

'Yes,' I say. 'I am.'

I notice that I'm the only person at the table not wearing glasses. And in fact I have met one of the others before. I met her yesterday. She works with Wei. It's embarrassing that I don't remember her name.

Wei and the man with long grey hair confer over the menu. They do so in Chinese, so I don't understand what they're saying, though sometimes they ask me whether I like certain things – pork, or shrimp.

'You're here to promote your book?' the grey-haired man asks me, while Wei puts the order in with the waitress.

'Yes,' I say.

'What sort of book is it?' he asks.

'It's a . . . it's kind of a history of Western civilisation.'

'Sounds interesting,' he says, making an effort.

'I hope so.'

'It's a big subject.'

'Yes, I couldn't fit everything in.' I decide to be flippant about it. 'There'll be some sequels. Keep me busy.'

He laughs politely. And then, with an amused smile, he says, 'What was it Gandhi said about Western civilisation . . .'

'That it would be a good idea?'

The man laughs again. 'Yes.'

'Actually I think that's apocryphal,' I say, sounding more defensive than I would have liked.

'Yes?'

'I think so.'

'I see,' he says.

The other people at the table are having a conversation in Chinese now.

'You're a writer as well?'

The man nods. He explains that his own books aren't published in mainland China, only in Taiwan and Hong Kong.

On the mainland it is possible, he tells me, to download his books for free from certain proscribed websites, and in fact this has been done hundreds of thousands of times.

'Well, that isn't much use to you,' I say, 'financially.'

'No,' he agrees. 'No.'

The first dishes arrive and we start to eat. There is a local specialty, roast pork with a thick, shiny reddish glaze under which is a generous layer of soft fat. The waitress watches us disapprovingly, I notice, as we start to tackle this. Finally, as if she can take it no longer, she steps forward and says something.

'She says we're eating it the wrong way,' the grey-haired man says to me.

'Oh?'

'We should eat it like this.' He makes a sort of mini sandwich out of a piece of the pork and one of the steamed buns that came with it, which we had initially ignored.

'OK.'

I go to take one of the glazed pieces of pork from the central dish at the same moment that Yaya does, the same piece. 'After you,' she says, in her totally American voice.

'No, go ahead,' I say.

'Thank you.'

She watches me, smiling, as I put together a pork sandwich, or try to.

'Have you seen the West Lake?' the older man asks me, just when I have my mouth full.

Wei overhears this. 'You're going to see it this afternoon, I think?' he says to me, while I swallow.

It was mentioned yesterday.

'Yes, I'd like to,' I say when I can speak again. I say it, however, in a tone that suggests it may not be possible. Because of the rain, I suppose I mean. And because I don't actually feel like sightseeing.

'You should see it,' Wei says. 'Yuning can take you.'

Yuning. That's the other young woman, the one I met yesterday, whose name I have forgotten twice already. I make an effort to fix it in my mind now. 'OK. Well, maybe we should see what the weather does?' This last remark I address directly to Yuning herself. It makes her laugh, for some reason.

The older man says, 'You know, there's a Chinese saying. A rainy lake is better than a sunny lake, but a foggy lake is best of all.'

'That's nice,' I say.

But Yaya says, 'I don't know that. I've never heard that.'

The older man doesn't seem to hear her. He is putting together another of the pork sandwich things.

'I've never heard that,' Yaya says again. 'Wei, have you heard that?'

17

Wei, as if not wanting to take sides, just smiles inscrutably.

And then Yaya says, to me, 'Anyway you have to see it. Maybe I'll come with you.' And I can't deny that this makes the idea more appealing.

✣

After the meal I wander off to find the toilet, which is out in the shopping mall somewhere, and when I get back to the restaurant Yaya seems to have left. Wei is just paying. 'So,' he says, putting his credit card back in his wallet, 'you'll go to the lake?'

'What do you think?' I ask Yuning, my tone sceptical.

'I think yes,' she says.

'What about Yaya? Does she want to come?'

Yuning looks doubtfully around, as if trying to find her. She obviously isn't there.

'She said she wanted to come,' I point out.

'I don't know where she went,' Wei says.

We are standing on the threshold of the restaurant, where its wooden floor meets the white floor of the shopping mall proper in a line that cuts diagonally across the patterns of both materials.

'What time is it?' I ask.

Wei consults his watch. 'It's nearly one thirty.'

'And what time do we need to meet later?' I ask. There is an event in the late afternoon. A lady is coming from Shanghai to interview me in front of an audience. What I most want to do in the hours until then is lie down in my hotel room. The idea of walking around in the rain all afternoon, and then probably having to go straight to the event, is exhausting and stressful.

'About five?' Wei says.

'How long does it take to get to the lake?' I ask. 'Is it far?'

'No,' he says, without hesitation. 'Not far.'

Somehow I can't find the strength or resolve just to say outright that I don't want to go. Partly because some dutiful part of me feels I should go, since I'm here, and see this thing that everybody seems so enthused about.

'And so what about Yaya,' I say, conceding at this point, I suppose, that we will in fact go. 'Didn't she want to come?'

'She's seen it before,' Yuning says, in a way that makes clear that she actually doesn't want Yaya to come with us.

'OK, but she said—'

'I'll let her know,' Wei assures me. He is one of those enviable people with beautiful manners, and it is perhaps natural for him to attribute to me, as my principal motivation, a fear of being rude. This fear is what he means to address, I think, when he says, 'Don't worry. I'll let her know that you've gone.'

✣

Outside, Yuning summons a taxi with an app on her phone. It only takes a few minutes to appear. Quite soon after that, though, we're stuck in traffic. This is frustrating for me because mainly I just want this expedition to be over as quickly as possible. When Wei said the lake wasn't far, I assumed he meant five, ten minutes in a taxi. Now when I ask Yuning how long it will take to get there, she says, 'Less than an hour, I think.'

At least that's what I think she said. I find it hard to understand her English sometimes.

Anyway, my heart sinks.

The rain is still coming down on the gathered, slow-moving traffic. I've never known rain so unvarying. For two days now it has been falling with the same relentless intensity.

I feel sleepy, even though I've only been up for a few hours.

'Did you try the craft beer at the thing last night?' I ask Yuning, after a long interval. There was this thing last night.

She seems to think about the question very earnestly for several seconds. Then she says, 'No.' She says it warily, as if it might be the wrong answer.

'It was quite good,' I say.

The taxi driver sighs at our lack of progress.

'Traffic seems heavy,' I say, a minute later.

'It's always like this,' Yuning says. She has a very pale oval face, a prominent underlip. A way of owlishly dipping her head when listening to someone, of looking out from under her hanging hair. There's a wryness to her sometimes.

I ask her some questions about her work – the job she does for the publishing company, in the IT department, or dealing with social media or something. The social media side, it seems to be, mostly. She says that isn't what she wants to do.

It turns out that she once lived in London, which surprises me. She was there for eight months, after finishing a degree (in what subject I don't know) at Exeter University. In London, she tried to find a job. She didn't, so she left. She says she would have liked to stay.

The lake appears as lakes do – water glimpsed through roadside trees. Thickening crowds on the waterside walks.

When we pull over, I find that I want to stay in the taxi. At least it's dry, and fairly warm.

Standing on the kerb, I put up the umbrella while Yuning pays the taxi driver.

Then the taxi drives away.

Now what?

The rain is falling without let-up.

I'm not sure what we're doing here.

At the place where we are a wide causeway strikes out across the lake and it seems like the obvious thing to do is to walk along it. That's what everyone else is doing.

Leafless trees line parts of the causeway. Their trunks and boughs are black, but the extremities of their branches are a dirty yellowish colour.

Business is slow for the boatmen. A few gondola-like boats are out on the water and it would be romantic, I suppose, in other circumstances, to do a boat ride in these conditions but when Yuning asks if we should do one, I say, 'Not today, I think.'

There's an ambiguity, already, about how close she has to keep to me to stay under the small umbrella. We keep softly knocking into each other as we walk along.

I maintain a brisk pace on the wet tarmac.

It's all grey, the view.

The islands and the hills on the distant shore.

The only things that aren't grey are the dead reddish-brown reeds in the shallows when the causeway arrives at an island.

'What's that?' I say. There's some temply thing among trees to the left. Yuning says she doesn't know. We go to look, passing through a circular gate. On the other side there's an inscribed stone, and I ask Yuning to translate the characters on it. In her long coat she leans forward, stiffly from the waist, like a hinge, to look at them.

'This is the place,' she says, taking care over her rendering of the Chinese, 'where you should see the moon over the quiet lake in autumn.'

The building whose gabled roof we saw above the trees is slightly offshore, linked to the main island by a circuit of little bridges.

The views from these bridges are very beautiful. Even the distant islands, veiled by the rain today, turned into delicate silhouettes, seem carefully placed on the surface of the lake.

The rightness of everything is captivating.

This is not just an accident. The whole landscape is

artificial. The lake itself is largely artificial. It wouldn't exist at all without damming and dredging, Yuning tells me as we stand there in the rain. The landscape of the lake, she says, is supposed to represent an idealised fusion between humans and nature. And standing there I find that it does indeed present a compelling image of an ideal. One that seems like a plausible basis for a civilisation. Plausible, but out of reach for us, I think, as a large tourist boat goes past, dragging its white wake. Because of how we see ourselves. We're down on ourselves. Us humans, I mean. We want to look in the mirror and like what we see. Whether we'll be able to do that, honestly, until we feel that we're living in something other than antipathy with the world around us seems unlikely. The rain patters on the umbrella. We are walking back along the causeway. When we arrive at the end there's a small crowd of people waiting for taxis and we attach ourselves to it. I hold the umbrella over Yuning while she uses her app. 'About ten minutes,' she says.

ENDURANCE: ONE HUNDRED YEARS AND ONE DAY LATER

Kamila Shamsie

SOON after we boarded the Russian icebreaker, *Polar Pioneer*, in Ushuaia, we were directed to meet at The Mustard Point. Surely the colour not the condiment, I thought, walking down the ship's corridors, which were unpromisingly lined with sick bags. Once outside I saw the rest of the passengers gathering next to hulking bullet-shaped objects that were clearly orange. No, not gathering – mustering.

The giant bullets were submersible lifeboats. In we climbed. Pressed together on benches, we listened to the expedition leader explain all the ways in which this vessel would keep us alive and safe if the *Polar Pioneer*, which was to be our home for the next ten days, ran into trouble and we were forced to leave. It's just as well I didn't know then that Shackleton's *Endurance* had set sail from South Georgia to Antarctica exactly one hundred years and one day ago, on 5 December 1914, and two days later first encountered the pack ice that would ultimately crush her. There were two lifeboats on the *Polar Pioneer* and about sixty of us divided between them. The word 'sardines' was the only one that would do – and that was before we were told that in the event of an actual evacuation the crew would join us, which would add another dozen or so people to each vessel. Then we were shown the bucket that would have to serve as 'the facilities' for the hours or days we were confined to the lifeboats. It was so awful to contemplate we passengers couldn't even hazard eye contact, let alone a joke.

Back out in the open, we watched South America recede; in time, the image of the bucket receded too. Ahead lay Antarctica – a word I had always vaguely associated with foolhardy men doing unnecessarily dangerous things that drove them to kill sled dogs, and sometimes eat them, in order to stay alive. I had never had a longing to go to the frozen wastelands of the earth – and yet when I was asked to do just that for a travel piece, something in my heart started singing. Who can understand the ways in which even the most urban among us can feel a pull towards the absolute unknown?

But when they tell you 'Antarctica' they skip over the 'Drake Passage' – a body of water that is the meeting point of the Atlantic and Pacific Oceans and the Southern Seas, made more remarkable by the fact that there is no significant landmass anywhere along its latitudes. No landmass means nothing to provide resistance to currents as they travel and grow in strength around the globe. What results are the world's choppiest seas. Or put in more visual terms: your view out of the porthole of the room in which you're lying prone on your bed is sky, sea, sky, sea. I don't mean a mix of sea and sky. I mean at one moment you are looking at nothing but sky and the next the porthole is covered with water. Repeat for thirty-six hours. The most surprising part of all this was how perfectly right it felt to be horizontal. Vertical was all wrong, but horizontal was fine, almost soothing. Stay horizontal, take seasickness pills, sleep, sleep some more.

Later, I understood the narrative necessity of the Drake Crossing. It wouldn't have been right to progress undramatically from Argentina to Antarctica on calm seas – the tempest-tossed voyage with its drug-induced drowsiness was an essential way of marking the passage from one world to another.

Because Antarctica really was another world. One pared down, pared back. There was sea and sky and icebergs and rocks. There were penguins and seals and petrels and skuas and occasionally whales. There were my fellow travellers and the ship's crew and the expedition staff. There was the *Polar Pioneer* and the inflatable Zodiacs. There was the morning expedition and the afternoon expedition. There was breakfast, lunch and dinner. There was sleep. There was landing on the continent and there was cruising between the icebergs. There was endless blue and endless white. There were layers and layers of clothes to put on and take off. There was my copy of *Moby Dick*. There was watching. There was talking, too, but most of it was about the day's watching – did you see the calving of the iceberg, the fluke of the whale, the line-up of gentoo and chinstrap and Adélie penguins, the blood-smeared slab of ice?

It was astonishing how quickly the world disappeared, how much I revelled in its disappearance. I too became pared down in what I was willing to absorb and with what I was willing to interact. Antarctica, *Moby Dick* and the people on the ship – that was as much as I could bear of the world. As early as day two, I wrote this in my journal: 'A note in the folder on the door tells me a complimentary email account has been set up for me. I can't imagine using it.' I never discovered how or where this email account was supposed to work on a ship – indeed, on a continent – where my smart-phone only functioned as a camera.

A couple of days later one of the passengers asked another a question and received the reply, 'I don't know, and I love that we can't google it.' Yes, exactly, I found myself thinking. There was a strange pleasure in returning to a state where so many things could be unknown. Tiny bits of trivia, the name of an actress, a quote from a book, the weather in some other part of the world, the causes of seasickness. The brain asked a question, cast about for an answer, realised, no, I don't know that and neither does anyone else standing around me – and there the matter rested. It was, I discovered, almost always fine not to have the answers to the questions that came and went from my mind; and on those occasions when it wasn't fine there was something so gloriously human in the wondering and wondering – what is the answer? How do I find it? How little I know.

When endless information isn't always at your fingertips, all new knowledge that comes to you from other people feels like a gift:

That crackling sound is air bubbles travelling to the surface of a piece of ice that has broken off a glacier; it is the sound of ancient air, perhaps 10,000 years old, escaping.

Penguins are heavy, like a small dog; seven or eight kilo-grammes, most of it blubber.

That glossy smooth texture of ice you see there – that's the mark of an iceberg melting in the sun.

In the pared-down world, even our actions were limited. All humans were visitors to Antarctica; the continent belonged to the animals and birds, and to nature itself. And as visitors there were strict rules about what we could do – we could not, for instance, approach a penguin, and if one approached us we were to move away and ensure we maintained a certain distance; we could not take anything – not a feather, not a pebble – from Antarctica. And we could leave nothing behind save for footprints that would soon disappear under snow.

The more the world became pared down, the more I saw the depth of its variety. So many shades of blue in the icebergs; so many textures of snow. So many icebergs to make you want to cry out with their sculptural beauty. Each whale sighting felt different, each glimpse of penguins transformed from land-waddling creatures to sea-torpedoes turned the world joyous.

The day I saw another ship far off in the distance I was furious. How dare anyone else exist in this world? The day I saw moss clinging to rocks I was distraught – we were returning northward to everything unnecessary, including the colour green. But my distress at these unwanted sights was nothing to the expressions I caught on the faces of the old Antarctic hands as they looked upon a strip of sand or a surface of rock they hadn't seen before in all their years of coming here. That sand, that rock, signalled melted ice, climate change.

'It's over for the Arctic, but Antarctica might still have a chance,' I heard one of the expedition guides say as I sat on the bridge one day reading *Moby Dick,* and glancing up from its pages to the snow petrels and ice-covered peaks all about. And for a moment right then I recognised what my low-grade but persistent sorrow at the thought of the journey's end was all about: I did not want to return to the world made by humans. Shackleton and his crew might have answered the question 'how much of Antarctica's hardship can men endure', but the weightier question remained: how much of humanity's arrogance will Antarctica – and everywhere – have to endure before we truly commit to course-correction? And where will we be relative to the point of no return when that occurs?

THE PART-TIME COUNTRYMAN
Max Porter

*T*HIS *train will be in reverse order, first class at the rear. There is no bicycle storage on this service, ladies and gentlemen, so if you are planning on taking a bicycle on this service we would ask you to wait for the delayed 08.23. We apologise for any inconvenience caused.*

The part-time countryman is a self-pitying creature. He cannot get his 'father' mask to fit.

Can't be bothered with office drinks. I've missed the last six tho! They'll take me off the email soon. See you in a bit. Xxx

There aren't any seat reservations, mate. You can sit anywhere.

He tells himself that he is an actor moving between stage sets. Persons in the workplace are props to be slid on and off stage, bit parts in his lonely professional drama. Likewise, his family, at home in the countryside, strike him as nothing more than representations, barely credible simulacra loved-ones, cardboard cut-outs from a catalogue of fake homeliness. But of course every day he returns home to find his beloveds are flesh and blood, noisy and needy, hungry and angry. And of course he arrives in the office every morning to find corporeal colleagues, chatting, groaning, working. So, day after day he must come to terms – bravely – with the fact that these people are all embodied and it is *he*, shuttling back and forth between the twin tableaux of capitalism and domesticity, it is *he* who is a cut-out to be slid on and off stage. He is forever his own understudy. When he performs well in one drama, he is nothing but central absence in another. His not-there-ness is what he is performing, day in, day out. His presence is a mirage. His absence is the only real thing about him.

> Luke: Spare room from day one.
> Tom: Spare room on weeknights.
> Nitin: Ear-buds and eye mask.
> Ed: Never changed a nappy.
> So, you get my point sweetheart, I'm kind of a hero. You might need to compare the market a bit before losing your rag. So can I or can I not go to the pub after cricket? X

There are no seat reservations, so it's *not* your seat, but if you're that stressed out I'll move to one of the many free seats.

The part-time countryman will forever be playing catch-up, and experiencing mild crises of identity. He should moisturise his face and hands regularly so that dry skin is never on his Worry List. Glycerine, shea and natural oils – well blended and over-priced – are the travelling man's friend.

My grandpa, on this train fifty years ago. My dad, on this train twenty-five years ago. I should've taken a gap year at least. I should've lived a bit more before settling down with Nicola.

But I'm all set to get promoted to SCS in five years, and I got a table seat with a plug socket tonight, so actually I can't complain.

30 Win. Win. Win.

Hi sweetheart, I missed the 18.30. On the 18.45. I'm really sorry about this morning. I was an idiot. You're right, I was too cross with the kids. I left the house 100% livid. I think I need to start cycling again. Anyway. See you in a bit. I'm starving btw. X

Keenly aware that his hands are filthy, he uses a lot of soap; he squeezes and squeezes and rubs the soap into the gaps between each finger, turns his hands over and does the backs of his hands, rubs his nails into his palms. He holds his hands under the tap but no water comes.

He waves his hands under the tap. He bends and checks to see if the electronic sensor is where he thinks it is. It is. There is no water.

He wipes the soap off with toilet paper. His hands are sticky.

This is the fourth time this has happened since he bought his season ticket in May.

The part-time countryman will need a sturdy briefcase, a bowler hat, a cane and a wry smile of matutinal solidarity for the milkman whom he will pass every morning. He will need wireless earphones and well-made socks. He should dismissively peruse the free paper and admire the lift and fall of Charlotte's breasts as she sighs over Instagram. He should stop naming familiar commuters as if he knows them, but come on, it's fun. He should stop looking at Charlotte's breasts, but come on, she's fit. He should peruse his emails – as if coolly unimpressed – but not reply to them. Shined shoes are not the integral sartorial component many mainstream gentlemen's periodicals will insist they are, and New Balance are verboten as everyone knows.

Like a baby in the womb, the part-time countryman should listen to classical music or language courses. If he develops a paunch, he must leave a little earlier, try a little harder to get a seat, and his briefcase will cover the bump.

31

To be honest love, it feels like a pretty raw deal, working as hard as I do, coming back to this, night after night. Thankless task, to be honest. Anyway. I'm not angry, just fed up. X

The part-time countryman must defecate in his countryside lavatory first thing in the morning and not in the metropolis. Never ever on the train. His colleagues in the city should imagine him dropping, as the sun creeps over the picturesque meadows, a healthier turd than theirs, a larger, better-built, half-country shit.

. . . *an assortment of hot and cold snacks, light refreshments and alcoholic beverages, but it is cash payments only this evening, ladies and gentlemen.*

The part-time countryman knows about pheasants, but he also knows about early mover premiums. He won the courgette category of the village show on his first attempt, but he also knows the best Japanese restaurant on Dean Street. He is a calibrated weapon of transition, of falsity and performance. The part-time countryman sees how business works, the arms and the heart and the daily stricken fleshy surface, and this is a burden. A well-cooked supper and some bracing expressions of gratitude can alleviate this burden. The part-time countryman plays knowingly at metrosexuality, but requires – and deserves – old-fashioned servicing.

All good?

All good, thanks mate.

Kids?

All good. Bit noisy for my liking. Your lot?

All good. Chloe's got a mobile phone.

Ha, mental. So it begins.

So it begins.

Thing is, you can track them. The kids. With the mobiles.

Yeah, I guess that's true.

Have a good one.

You too, mate.

The part-time countryman must remember that children are buoyant and respond to almost every imaginable psychological strain better than adults do, even well-paid and recently promoted adults with expensive shoes. Children must be steered to recognise and appreciate the kaleidoscopic duties of their parents, whilst also being shown tactics of adaptation and survival, and also being left to their own devices to hunt, or download apps. They will engage with livestock, they will adopt local superstitions and find their own paths to friendship and, later, romance. Children are intrepid in ways the part-time countryman will find startling and possibly threatening. He should anoint the hinges of his squeaky personality with the carefree natural oil of childhood curiosity. He will soon find his child's easy manner is his own, and he will be liked for it. As a city chap he should be able to understand this: what is a child if not a verifiable asset?

> I don't know what's going on, love. I locked myself in the loos and cried. I mean I properly cried, bent double heaving. I think I might need to talk to someone. I'm not sure who I am. X

> All good?
> All good, mate. You?
> All good. Could do with a seat.
> Tell me about it.

> PS Sorry. Xxx

The part-time countryman realises that generalisations about the character of country and city are useless for those slung halfway between. He bridles at the description of a businessman, and seeks to take his informed hammer to clichés of the rural community. He has a hidden sense of time, lacks pettiness and is painfully self-aware, but this makes him god-like in both his spheres, with a penchant for impersonation. He plays the village like a game on his phone. He can imitate the squeamish aversion of city folk to livestock with uncanny skill because he was once that nose-pinched newcomer. He can mock the misguided sentimentality of a city visitor's misty-eyed appreciation of 'beauty' because he in fact daily feels the fresh amazement of the picturesque even as he has to shrug it off in order to belong. Cultivated and flexible duplicity, enriched with snobbery, is the part-time countryman's sharpest weapon in the theatrical war of his own existence.

> Yes, I phoned the train company and asked them to cancel the 17.30 especially so I could miss dinner with your parents.

There's something about us all standing in the aisles waiting, while the train idles outside the station, waiting for a platform, all of us stood up, coats on, cases at the ready, little tuts and smiles and shrugs. There's something about this that is the saddest thing in the world. The seventeen-year-old me, still seated, looking up at me like wow you really walked where the path doesn't tread, didn't you?

I always look up at the exact same moment. Maybe it's a ley line. Straight view through the valley, golden. No filter. I'm not big into the gazing out of the window, but I always look up at this same place, take it all in. Feel small.

> I'm so bored, babe. I'm just so bored. X

The part-time countryman seeks, whether he knows it or not, one significant asset above all others, one permanent prize: respectability. He wishes most of all to be looked squarely in the eye by his neighbour in the country, to be seriously appreciated, to be heard on important issues. For if he is not respected he is silly. Silly fool, silly twat, silly billy. Silly covers every aberration from ill-advised clothing to genuine lunacy, and the village will unite behind the word silly and use it to banish into otherness the pitiful part-time countryman who could not be respected.

I'm in trouble for saying Angie was shrill. You can't say anything these days. Hashtag sorryforbreathing. Laters x

Hi mate, me again, about the pool skimmer. Sorry to leave another message but we're just hoping it's turned up? It's just Amazon said they definitely delivered it to our safe place, and Megs definitely saw your little fella in our shed, which is the safe place, and there's the little rip section of the package on the floor, and obviously I'm not wanting to accuse him of anything, but it's just a pool skimmer, so if there's any way you could just sort of ask him again, that would be wicked, we'd be massively grateful, alright, nice one, speak soon, cheers.

I'm on level 300 on Candy Crush. I've listened to every single Adam Buxton podcast. Can do the Killer Sudokus in five minutes. I've got a Kindle loaded up with Mark Billinghams. I'll be all right.

I told Henry Atkins that I regularly fantasised about throwing myself in front of the hi-speed, and now he avoids me on the platform. Don't be scared, Henry, I won't take you with me.

Respect. This is what he thinks about as he slips into sleep, when his daytime worries have been set aside. Respected in the pub, respected in the field, respected in the bedroom. A proper modern man.

Hi love. Missed the 18.30. Sorry I'm angry in the mornings. I'm not sure where I belong. I'll man up, I promise. X

STATE OF EMERGENCY
Sara Collins

WE loaded the car and drove into the hills. We packed the radio, because we needed it; and nappies, because we needed them, too. We took fifty US dollars per head, which the law allowed us, but not much else, because this is the story of the things we didn't carry and, since it was Jamaica in 1977, we didn't carry much. By this time the State of Emergency was already seven months old; there had been an outbreak of political violence in the lead up to the elections – the beginning of a long national nightmare – and my parents decided we had to leave.

The prime minister, Michael Manley, had promised to smash capitalism 'brick by brick', and I guess you could say we were getting hit by all those flying bricks. We drove all night, until below us the place we'd come from was nothing but a black shadow sinking into the sea, caught in the first glaze of sunrise, and, even though we loved that old landscape and all its green undulations, we didn't look back. We were ironing ourselves out of it, getting the hell away.

I want to tell you how, after you've left a place this way, you may find yourself needing to write about it, keeping in your rearview a litany of things you don't remember, with as much choice in these things as you might have about falling in love. How when you start writing, you'll find yourself coming full circle to the same emergency. The same words leaping around you eager as dogs: curfew-gunman-garrison-gun. How I read books because those words were caught in my head like a line from a song.

÷

We flew to Grand Cayman: my parents, my three brothers and I. We got ourselves a room of our own. Two beds, two crocheted bedspreads, one bassinet. My Caymanian grandmother, whose house it was, had a habit of jabbing at my skin like it was something she forgot in the oven. 'You caught the sun,' she'd say, as we both surprised ourselves with the discovery that she'd have loved me better pale. My mother worked night shifts. During the day my brothers and I tried to prise her eyelids open while she slept. I stared at myself in the mirror with her nurse's badge pinned to my T-shirt and her white cap perched on my afro, imagining what it would be like to be a woman who worked. One of our neighbours, a man named McDoom, who ran a bar called Club Inferno in a place called Hell, brought us gifts of food. Baskets of yams. Green bananas.

Finally we could afford the rent on one half of a shared duplex, where one night we built a bonfire in our backyard and my brothers and I raced each other around it, thin and barefoot, singing: Run from Michael Manley! Run from Michael Manley! We were finding our feet (limping, yes, but standing), my father working again as a barrister, picking up the threads of his old life, so we could afford to fill an old barrel every couple of months. Packs of Jacob's cream crackers scuttled like crabs under lace-edged underwear (the 'good' kind that wouldn't shame you before the eyes of ambulance-drivers), Johnson & Johnson talc, bags of cornmeal, tins and tins of sardines. The barrel would stand in a corner of the kitchen filling up slowly until the lid sat snug on the final item – perhaps a navy-blue tin of Danish butter cookies – and then it would be dispatched to my Jamaican grandmother, who was one of the things we'd had to leave behind.

÷

You could spend too much time trying to understand what led to those hardscrabble years, but it boils down to the same story everywhere, doesn't it? The machinations of men. I understood nothing at the time about what we were doing or why we were doing it. I was a child and these were not childish matters. The PNP and the JLP were at war and it turned out there wasn't enough country for the both of them. It turned out there's no such thing as an easy passage.

In April 1978, there was a concert in Kingston – the One Love Peace Concert – an attempt to stitch the two sides together, would-be murderers with would-be murderees: Bob Marley on stage, joining the hands of the two reluctant leaders, the two pale kings – Manley and Seaga – buckra men in a country that had taught itself those were the best kind of men to be. Bob telling the people to come together. And maybe for a moment they all believed him, they believed in the possibility of peace, they left behind the light poles and dirt patches and bullet-wounded walls of the old garrisons. There was a frenzy of dancing; they seemed happy as cult members. Bob telling them that things would be all right. You could almost believe it, too, if you went and watched it now, if you didn't already know the future, if you didn't know that sometimes it seems the State of Emergency was the only thing that lasted. By the date of the peace concert, I was already gone, already watching the unfurling of a country that would never belong to me.

÷

Jamaica was the place that had caused all this. It was seven years before we could go back to visit. Summer. A break from school. All six of us in the rented car. Twisting this way and that for a backseat view of the things we had abandoned, noticing everywhere these quick currents of memory I couldn't quite grasp. There were so many things around me I didn't know that I'd forgotten. The car pushing inch by inch through street vendors, who cried out and waved bags of just-roasted peanuts, peppered shrimp, fried fish and bammies. Their hands slipped like fishes past the glass. I had never seen this kind of urgency to sell something before, this way of pushing the thing at you, so you had to take it or be hit with it.

We started going uphill: urgent noises from the clutch and engine. After a time there seemed to be a bar or church every hundred yards; then women, straddling the roadside with children on their hips, who, when they heard the car, stopped and shifted to the side, without looking around. But sometimes there was no one for miles. Only the orange groves, or the small, ramshackle, apparently deserted buildings. Wood, zinc, sturdier houses sitting proudly beside concrete cisterns. Corner shops. Burglar grilles. Chain-link fence after chain-link fence.

Then, finally, Lambsriver. My grandmother's tiny flat-roofed house: the walls blue-green inside and out; the floor that thumped underfoot; the yellowing crocheted curtains; the smell of wood. She came out onto her porch, plaits battened down under a head-tie, and watched at arm's length as we poured ourselves out of the car. We were shy of each other, but my brothers and I trailed her through her garden. Breadfruit and mango and banana. More trees than flowers. We followed her to the outside kitchen, leaving all our questions hanging. A pot of goat meat ticked away on the stove. She'd baked toto, and as usual with anything that delicious we gave each other the eye, the starting signal for our usual backwards race to be last to finish, and, after we had, we peeled mangoes with our teeth and threw the skins into a pile under the tree, raising up a cloud of flies. We took our long, brainless pleasure in the food. I liked the way this grandmother looked at me. As if I was something you could be proud of. Then we heard our mother calling out urgently from the house: 'What is all this? What is all this?' And when we rushed inside we found her standing dumbstruck before Grandma's wide-open wardrobe, pulling out bars of unused Ivory soap, tins and tins of talcum powder. Cotton nighties unfolding like white birds. My grandmother watched my mother from the doorway and, when her smile came it came slowly, like something that had been waiting a long time to be seen.

✧

I want to tell you how lonely it must have been, to be the one left behind, curating the contents of those barrels, waiting to show us when we came.

✧

How each person's perseverance is only after all the simple matter of an accumulation of breaths.

✧

How these small acts of perseverance hardly ever add up to something history cares two figs about.

✧

How we left her that day, too, and drove back down to our hotel, and my brothers and I squeezed onto the concrete balcony and elbowed our way to the railing, so we could perch on the bottom rung and look out across the sand and whisper about the tourists, glossy with tanning spray, beating back against the currents of dark water swelling around their waists.

✧

How that last image is a palimpsest. Faint beneath it are men on ships, and fainter still the traces of all the bad things that followed them.

✧

How sometimes I hate the whole notion of endurance, mainly because it is the trick that hoodwinks us into staying in place.

✧

How breath is the only tool with which we fight extinction.

✧

For a long time I didn't have the money or time to return, but, ten years afterwards, I travelled the Caribbean with a friend. Jamaica was on our list. We hitched a lift from Kingston to Montego Bay and waited in town for the Lambsriver bus. Shabba Ranks blared from a nearby sound system and I wandered over to a cart offering cigarettes for sale, negotiated a Benson & Hedges and a lit match from the woman tending it, standing to one side away from the crowd to smoke, wondering if anything would ever stop me feeling always and forever a visitor everywhere, but especially here.

A slight, dark, gap-toothed man slotted himself into the space between cart and wall and hugged the cigarette-seller from behind. She kissed her teeth. 'What you troubling me fah? You nah see me working?'

But he spun around, addressing himself to the small crowd of us leaning against the wall. 'You see this woman? Me love her bad, you see! Me love her bad!'

You couldn't help but grin, and when I looked at the woman she was smiling too.

My friend and I, the people leaning against the wall, the music, the cigarette-seller's lover, the way she laughed, leaning over the cart towards him, like she was peering into the bathroom mirror to paint her face. Here was a country. The place where, for me, desire had outlived memory. I felt my love for that whole place stir then; I felt love, like breath, conspiring with muscles and lungs and heart. I felt it as a thing harder to endure even than the history that had led to it.

My friend and I took the bus to Lambsriver. My grand-mother had sprained her wrist, but she'd still been cooking all morning. I made her sit at the table and, as I tied a makeshift sling across her shoulder, she spread the fingers of her good hand wide across the wood and seemed happy. I would have known what to say to her had the country not snapped itself in two, leaving her on one side and me on the other. I had one of those cardboard disposable cameras with me and I took a picture of her before I left, a snapshot that could not yet reach across the space and time between that moment and the one when I would find myself, about ten years later, driving slowly through her village, knowing that she was dying, when my memory of her sprained wrist and her joy about the sling would rear up at the sight of her little house, and I'd sit beside her holding her hand and trying to conjure up some important thing to say, when the woman my mum was paying to look after her rattled the Dutch pot in the sink as if impatient to see the back of me and it would strike me that it was too late for the thing I wanted: Gran's approval, or at the very least, her forgiveness. As if guilt was the only thing I had to show after going out into the world, and coming back.

ARIADNE
Daisy Johnson

A HOUSE
—

Y mother has wandering hands and a restless body. She drags us between cities, on and off trains. The grass is always greener on the other side. She likes new things. When I was a toddler I grew used to the labyrinth of wine bars and pubs, to creeping beneath tables and lingering beside the swaying legs. I can find her in any room; I know the smell of her. She will not look for me but I will look for her. Each birthday she paints her face and bakes a cake that tastes of spice and too much lemon. I think she counts the days until I am old enough to fend for myself. She likes to blow out the candles together, counting down; she likes to tell me stories about her own wild teenage years. I think my father must be buried somewhere in the midst of them, staring out at me from all the other faces. His body looks a lot like hers and when he smiles he has her careful, doubting eyes. I see her, in spring, growing bored. She sits out on the stoop of our rented house until it gets dark. She chops her hair and leaves the enormous, lion's tail of it in the sink. By summer we are on the move again. She buys me things but does not speak apologies. The train croissants dry my mouth out. She says the city we are going to has a wall almost all the way around it and a beautiful cathedral. I have seen it I have seen it I have seen it. On my birthdays I eat a cake with spice and too much lemon juice and I count each year until I am free. The house we roll up to has long solemn eaves crusted with old swallow's nests and a narrow-shadowed garden churned by the roots of an oak.

ANEW

M Y mother has always known how to bring love to her. In the summer storms drenched men come confused and frowning to our door saying they are lost and do not know where they are. In the mornings the postman stays for longer than it takes to deliver a letter. The galley kitchen smells of turmeric and babies' breath. The long wooden table is already scarred with chopping and stained with juice from the herbs she has set growing. In the evenings the smell of her margaritas is strong enough to burn a clean path through the magic. She is gentler then. We watch cooking shows until late, her long legs on my lap. Sometimes she asks me to paint her toenails or plait her hair. I am undone by her. I see how it must be when she makes eye contact with someone in the bookshop or leans across to touch a barman's arm. I see how everything about her says: I mean trouble and, also, I am for you. She makes me drinks but I will not have them. She is my mother but I keep my guard up by my face. I keep my wits about me. I watch her and so I know when she has met someone new, someone different. The kitchen smells like melted butter and she sings in the shower and as she gets ready. I watch the late-night cooking shows alone. She comes back almost speechless, seemingly undone. She strokes my hair. She stops chopping herbs and puts away her pestle and mortar. She bakes instead. The tall house is lifted with the smell of fresh bread, pastries. She puts on happy weight around her hips. She comes to my bedroom and stands in the doorway talking. She tells me she likes the material I have hung over the lamp, the colours I have painted the walls from old tester pots. I wait for her to turn. This house does not know us but I feel it waiting too.

AGAIN
—

THIS city was beautiful in the summer, but in the winter it turns hard. My neck hurts from watching my back. There is barely the relief of snow, only layers of ice over everything. The pipes burst and flood the kitchen. The turn I have been waiting for in her comes like the freeze. She berates the man who comes to fix the plumbing and will not pay him. She gets someone in to tear down the oak tree. I see her out there at three in the morning – stark by night-light – planting knobbly bulbs in the overturned dirt left from the torn-out tree. The windows of the house steam over and never seem to quite clear. She takes long, raging baths. I do not see her eat. I will not say that she sleeps. She locks herself in her room and I do not see her for months. She fills the air and I find myself scratching at the skin on my arms, sitting bolt upright in the night. I put on my coat and walk in the dead streets, through the gutted parks, the river like a black hole through the city. The walls close in around me. I know that at night she rages through the kitchen, eating everything that I buy. I never seem to be able to catch her at it, though sometimes the house trembles as she passes through, the shudder of her footsteps as if she has grown enormous. One night I am woken by her howls. They are sounds to wake the dead. The corridor feels full of hauntings. I bang my hands against her door but she only wails as if torn apart. I sit on the floor and wait for it to end and – at some point – there is silence. I listen. The heating has long broken and I can see my breath like mercury in the air in front of my face. I hear something. Or think I do.

A REPRIVE

—

SHE comes back to me the way she always does. My seasonal mother. We read in her favourite bars or on benches in still-chilly parks. She tests me on my chemistry and philosophy. My birthday comes and – looking at her – I see not impatience but love, perhaps. A love made of hammers and nails. She makes friends with a butcher and brings home more meat than we can fit in the freezer. She likes them animal-like still: the ducks with their long, broken necks, the cloven pig hooves, the prairie oysters she likes fried on a chilly dawn. When she moves to hold me her pulse seems exuberant, inexhaustible. I know that she wants me wild and wilful as she but there is not room for two of us the same. I find myself drawn to quiet moments, to silent films and empty rooms. She laughs at me. In the night I think I hear scratching in the walls or in the attic above me. I tell her squirrels might have got in off the roof and she says she'll find someone to sort it but never does. I do not think to berate her. How could I when she is the way she is, her bare shoulders, the cup of coffee she brings me in the morning, her fingers stained with blackberry juice?

ANOTHER

—

SOMETHING is wrong here. I wake again and again in the night. The meat supplies in the fridge dwindle as if my mother is midnight feasting though she laughs and says she isn't. The ground once riddled with oak roots now grows a thick fur of poppy, the red heads tearing beneath my feet. The windows in the house sometimes shiver in their frames. There is a smell of mushroom-rot from the drains. A toilet blocks and when I work the blockage free I find a tangle of dark hair, thicker than a human's, knotted to clumps. The squirrels – or rats – in the attic writhe and rocket around. My mother only tilts her head back onto the sofa and says she hears nothing. There are bruises on her arms and when she laughs at me I see a tooth is missing from her white smile. I do not ask her. I have never asked and got a simple answer. I wait for an evening when she, restless once more, says that she will go out. I help her pile her hair on top of her head. She says she'll be back late, if at all. The house rings with her absence. There is a dusting of gold on my hands from her makeup. I press it to my face to try to steal some of her fearlessness. Something in the attic rolls and moans. I take the stairs two at a time. If I let myself I will be too afraid and do nothing. The smell from the attic is familiar. I do not turn on the light and something rocks and clicks in the darkness, skirting away from me. I get down on hands and knees. In the darkness something touches my hand. I am fearless I am fearless I am fearless. Something croons or cries. I feel its wet mouth on my skin.

A LOVE

—

I HAVE been angry at my mother before. Sometimes I think we are connected by a thread of rage towards one another. The time she cut her hair and then, hating it, cut mine to match. The stray schools I went to where she would appear to pick me up and I would watch her ranging through the fathers, jackal-hungry, never more wanting than

49

when there was something she couldn't have. The things she has said. The things I see passing over her face when she looks at me. I have been angry at my mother before but never in such a way as this. I have loved before. I love her often and enormously. I have loved people I've seen in the street, flashes of wanting: a woman with kind eyes, a man with long fingers. I have loved houses we've lived in, the tight corners, the different smells. I have loved before but never like this.

A SECRET

—

THE creature I find in the attic does not trust me and will not come close. He hates the light and screams if I turn it on. I gain an image of him from flashes of vision and touch. He is small and skinny, all ribs and ballooning belly. He smells like an animal, like the cattle on the farm my mother worked at – begrudgingly – for a season. His head seems too heavy for his shoulders and tips forward so that often – in the moments of light – I cannot see his eyes. His head is matted with hair and buried beneath are two sore nubs of bone protruding from the skull. I sneak away whenever I can and sit with him. He grows used to me. He has been in the dark all his life and so he uses his soft, damp nose and his mouth to feel his way around. Sometimes when he tastes my hand I think he can tell what I am thinking. When I am angry he rages too and I have to make myself small in a corner. When I am tired he sleeps and sleeps. Even in the cold dark I think I sense something of my mother in him, but at times I feel him losing sense of himself and then I am afraid. He clamps both hands over my arms and holds on tight. He grovels on the floor and reaches for fragments of bone left over

50

from the meat she has been feeding him and grinds them between his teeth until they are dust. And then, again, he becomes calmer and we sit together listening to the swallows chittering through the walls. He does not speak but sometimes I do, quietly, and he makes sounds as if he understands what I am saying.

AN ESCAPE

—

HE will not speak but I have taught him one knock for yes, two for no. I bring him mice I catch in traps in the garden. I tell him everything I can about the world and the way I have lived in it so far. I tell him the plots of all the films I have seen. When my mother drinks we lie with our faces pressed to the dusty floor and listen to her smashing glasses in the kitchen. I tell him all the dreams I can remember. When I run out of things to say I let him put his tongue against my wrist. The sound of my pulse seems to calm him. I catch moths in jam jars with candles as lures and let them loose into the attic. He seems to like the sound of their busy wings in the darkness. I fill wine glasses with water and run my fingers around them to make them sing. It calms him to hear the sound. Some days my mother has new bruises or he won't let me near him, howls and comes at me with his teeth. I find that cutting the soft pads of my thumb and letting the blood drip into his mouth brings him a degree of peace when he is at his wildest. I plan how to escape with him: I tell him about places I have heard of but not been to. He likes the sound of their names: *Tasmania, Louisiana, Paris*. I dream that we live in the sewers and drains beneath cities and come out at night. We live off takeaways frightened from the arms of delivery boys.

AN END

—

MY mother starts scattering her sentences with signs. She talks about getting someone in to kill the squirrels in the roof or doing the job herself. Once or twice I wake and she is standing over me, wild-haired and fist-handed, her nightdress glowing white in the gloom. Let's eat cow tonight, she says, and I feel so afraid for him I sleep at the foot of the attic stairs. She never says: I know that you know. And neither do I. She never says: I see you've met your brother. We exist in the spaces between words, the silences when neither of us speaks. I catch mice by the dozen. I fill the bottom of a glass with blood and feed it to him. I say: when you grow strong – when you are better – when you aren't afraid any more. He knocks his hoof-hand hard against the floor, once, twice, once again. What do you mean? I say and he knocks again twice, once, once again. What are you trying to say? But he is silent.

AMAZE

—

WE do not sleep. The lights in all the rooms blaze out the windows onto the streets. The cathedral weeps its bell song. There is the stench of boiled thistles and the sap from cedar trees. My mother's arms are wrapped in silk she has ripped from her wardrobe, her hair has gone white overnight and her eyes are the colour of bees. I down coffee and play music loud but she seems to run on air alone. My brother wails and we no longer pretend we do not hear him. There is something growing in the garden, out in the torn earth where the oak tree stood. The dirt seeps water and our bare feet churn it to mud. Out of the wreckage corn is growing straight and strong and golden. The sound of her running her silk-wrapped fingers through it is a death rasp, a glottal stop. The corn grows in strict rows. I do not see it for what it is until I look out of my bedroom window and, peering down, understand what she is growing out in the garden. The higher the corn grows the more afraid I become. When I look down from my bedroom window I see that the maze does not only fill the garden but moves down beneath the soil, a rabbit tunnel of dead ends and no-ways-out. What are we doing here? How can we live this way? We tear the life from one another. We birth cattle from our raging bodies. My mother teaches me to drink in the herb-ripe kitchen. I lick the salt from the bridge of her hand. She holds a bottle between her thighs and pulls the cork. She will tell me soon whom the maze is meant for. If she chooses him I do not know if I will have the courage to offer myself in his place. I imagine dirt in my mouth and in my lungs, the dry seizure of the corn growing above my head. I imagine my skin becoming clogged with new-growth hair, my skull sprouting the horns I will soon grow.

THE DEPARTURE
Tash Aw

M Y father left for Singapore when I was about four years old. Of course, I can't remember anything about his departure, though over the years I've convinced myself that I was witness to certain things that happened on the day he left. For example: that he left his bus ticket in the kitchen and had to rush back to get it, but when he got home my mother had already gone to work, and he had to break into the house to retrieve it. It was late at night, my mother had just started a job as a cleaner at a fish wholesaler down the road, and I had been asleep for a few hours. When my father broke the latch on the window it disturbed the dog in the yard next door, which began to bark. It was a thin mongrel the colour of sand, old and half-blind, and maybe because it was slow and couldn't see anything it got spooked easily and barked at the slightest noise. I remember it well: eyes like glass marbles that seemed as though they might pop out of their sockets at any moment. You may think the dog is an incidental detail in this story. But I can remember it so clearly that it makes the rest of that evening seem real in my memory.

I woke up and started to cry in the dark. My father was startled; he couldn't bear the wailing, so he started to come into the bedroom to comfort me, but he knew that if he picked me up and held me until I was calm again he would miss his bus – and all chances of decent work and money would disappear, and he would have to go back to gutting fish at the factory on the other side of Kuala Selangor.

It was raining heavily. The sound of the rain drumming on the tin roof, normally so soothing, that night agitated me, and I sat up in bed, blinking and sobbing in the dark. Outside: the barking dog, the yard turning to mud. My father stood in the doorway, staring at me. He'd been caught in the rain: his clothes were dripping and left patches of water on the linoleum that my mother would find when she came home some hours later. He'd been in a hurry; he hadn't had time to take his shoes off and ended up leaving muddy tracks all over the floor. He stood watching me for a while, then left. The sound of my crying followed him out of the house, all the way into the rainstorm as he boarded the night bus headed south.

I wish I could tell you that I remember him standing at the doorway, or that I could hear his breathing, heavy and rushed because he had been running. But the likelihood is that I started to cry because I'd had a bad dream and woke up for a few seconds before falling asleep again. It must have been those nightmares that only children have, where sleep and awakeness and dreaminess and reality get entangled before evaporating into a cloud that hangs over them for hours, so that even when they're awake, they're really still asleep, still dreaming. You and I – we don't have this muddledness. Everything is distinct. Work time. Play time. Eat time. Sleep time. I don't know how this change takes place in someone's life, but it does, overnight, and they don't even know it. I'm not sure how it happened with me – I just woke up one morning and thought, hurry up, it's time for work now. I was fifteen years old. And that beautiful cloudiness on waking from slumber that I remembered from my childhood, sometimes sad, sometimes comforting – it had just vanished.

The story of my father coming home in the rainstorm to retrieve his bus ticket was told and retold to me by my mother numerous times over the years, until the images of my father that evening became so sharp and true that I believed I had seen them myself. She repeated the story frequently – so often that I thought: she wants me to believe that he cared for me. I cried; he wavered. Back then we still believed that he would be coming home to us, and when he finally did we would have more money and life would be easier. My parents were still in contact, more or less on a regular basis. A letter would arrive from Singapore from time to time, a single sheet of thin paper with a rough edge where it had been torn from a notebook. You'd think that he could have at least bought decent paper to write on. My mother would read the few lines so intently you'd think it was the I Ching or some special advice sent to her by Confucius himself. Sometimes she'd read just one line aloud, slowly and seriously, like a newsreader announcing a disaster. '*Singapore Is Very Clean.*' Or, '*Here, Spitting Is Not Allowed,*' or '*No One Has To Pay Bribes Here.*' I have no idea what else he said to her in those letters – everything was just condensed into those single lines, a public broadcast message.

A few times, we walked to Ah Heng's sundry store half a mile away to wait for a phone call from my father, which I guess he must have promised in a previous letter. Only the calls never came through. Who knows why – maybe he had to line up for too long to use the phone at the warehouse where he worked, or maybe he had to work overtime, or maybe he just forgot. How did people live without mobiles? Maybe you're too young to remember pay phones, maybe not. It seems like only yesterday, but life was so different. It seems strange now to think about how much time we wasted at Ah Heng's place. Hours and hours hanging around for that call which never came.

To hide the embarrassment and pain of that fruitless

waiting, my mother pretended that we needed to go to the shop to buy things. I'd sit on the sacks of rice, filling the time by memorising the way the various things were arranged on the shelves, then closing my eyes and reciting them until I got the order right. *Mumm 21. Shelltox. Maggi Mee Perencah Kari.* There was never very much stock, and what there was never changed position – biscuits, diapers, flour. Everything stayed where it was, covered in a thin film of dust. If I close my eyes now I can see every single object on those shelves, and I bet if you went there tomorrow, they would still be on the same metal shelves, arranged in exactly the order I've told you. My mother would chat to Ah Heng about all sorts of things, giving him news about my father, which wasn't actually news because it was the same set of facts repeated every time: he had a new job; he was sending money home; he would come back soon and we would either build ourselves a new house somewhere in the Sekinchan area or move to Klang. Either way we would stop living in the house we lived in then – half wood, half cement – because the wood was rotting and my mother was tired of patching up the gaps between the planks with pieces of biscuit tins that she flattened out with a hammer. She seemed to spend a lot of time doing this, but new holes were always appearing – spots of white light, brilliant as stars. She couldn't keep up with them; nature was stronger than she was. We had to move. I would need my own room; I couldn't go on sharing with my parents. With my *father–mother*. She spoke as if we were a family, a normal, proper family, because that's what we were, in her head and in mine, and probably in Ah Heng's and in everyone else's too.

When she talked about the life we were going to have, it all made sense. It seemed connected to where I was, sitting on the sacks of rice; it was part of the same story, a story of waiting, of waiting for things to get better, because they would. We all thought we knew how the story would turn out, because why would it turn out any other way? My father was in Singapore, he was earning a decent wage in a warehouse in a country that had rules about employment, where he got paid in full on the same day each month – a detail that seems so small and irrelevant as I talk about it now, but back then seemed so important to us that it was worthy of being boasted about. *Every month, without fail – no arguing, nothing, he gets his salary*. I can remember my mother saying this to Ah Heng one day.

Of course it was all fake; our lives weren't getting any better. If they were, we would have been buying more than just a packet of cornflour or a single coconut, which Ah Heng would split in two and scrape out in his old machine which consisted of a big metal bowl and a spinning metal head. We would have been buying tins of Danish butter cookies, going out for meals in seafood restaurants; I would have had a new school uniform that fit me, that wasn't four sizes too big because it had been bought to last me through the rest of primary school. Maybe a holiday – not anything fancy like a week all-inclusive in Bali or a coach tour of Thailand that people do nowadays, but just some time away, on the other side of the country, visiting relatives in Penang or staying with my aunt in Kampar and spending a few days eating chicken biscuits. All the things that a normal family would do. How much could a bus ticket have cost back then? Even now it only costs twenty ringgit, max. We could have done all that if my father had actually been sending money through to us.

That was when I realised my mother's stories were intended not to comfort me, but to reassure herself. The more she repeated the stories to me and Ah Heng and whoever else cared to listen, the clearer it was to me that she needed to cling to the belief that it was all true – that my father was still part of our lives, that our future was bright, and soon we would be living on the outskirts of Klang, in one of those new housing estates that were being built – just like the one we're sitting in now.

These days, it's difficult to imagine anyone actually dreaming of living in this area. The houses all look shabby now – no one wants to live in these tiny single-storey places any more. The people who are here wish they were living somewhere else. Secretly they all want to be in KL or Petaling Jaya. The drains outside the houses are blocked up by rubbish and dead leaves; the grass on the edge of the roads is over-grown and messy – the council doesn't bother to clean up stuff on the streets around here. There used to be small gardens in front of the houses; now there are only cars, old Proton Sagas crammed into the concrete yards. A few doors down there's an old couple who use their Perodua as a kind of outdoor cupboard. At first you think it's just another small lousy old car, then you realise it's full of clothes and boxes and unwanted stuff like that. The neighbours – we see each other around and sometimes we say hi, sometimes we don't. I like it that way. No one asks me any questions.

But it wasn't supposed to be this way. When this neigh-bourhood was built, I remember looking at the tiled roofs and thinking, woah, they look so solid. In some other estates the houses have blue roofs, some have green. My mother cut out an advertisement from the *Sin Chew Jit Poh* with a drawing of a house just like this one. Far from the sea, where we wouldn't have to smell the salty, stinky mud when the tide went out, full of rotting fish that slipped out from the nets of the fishing boats. A house far inland, that couldn't be swept away by freak tides or floods or storms. A place close to the city – so near that you could feel part of it, be absorbed and protected by it. She pinned the piece of newspaper to the wall in the bedroom – a patch of colour against the bare board. These places, they felt so new, even beautiful. It's hard to remember that sense of wonder now. You drive around this kind of estate and the streets look identical, house after house after house – they're all the same, it crushes you. I know that's what people from KL think. You come from the big city and you think, these places destroy your soul. Even I feel like that sometimes, and I've lived here for nearly ten years. I don't know how things could have changed so much in thirty years. The houses we dreamt of then are exactly the ones we live in today, but they belong to a different world.

I used to wonder how my parents felt about each other during that long period of separation and waiting to be with each other again – those long years of hope. Sometimes we used to watch *Shanghai Tang* on TV, that Hong Kong series that had just come out then, which everyone was watching. We loved the costumes, the glamour – and that song! It made my mother cry every time. Once, she dabbed her eyes and said, 'It must be beautiful to experience such things. To be in love like that.' And then, as if she heard the question that was forming in my head, she said, 'It's different for people like us. Your father and me, we don't have time for all that.'

Over the years, I've often thought about what she said. *Didn't have time for love.* Is that what she meant? They were apart from each other, romance was impossible, I understand that. But love – that's something else, isn't it? My father was in another country earning a living far from his family, but that was another form of love. Distance is love. Separation is love. Loneliness is love.

One day – I can't remember when, but I was older then, a few years after my father left for Singapore – we received a letter from him. My mother read out a couple of sentences as soon as she opened the envelope. '*I have been going to church for the past few months.*' '*The pastor says that my life will improve because Jesus loves me.*' She stood reading for a minute or so, then took the letter into the bedroom and shut the door. I can't remember exactly how the rest of the information filtered through to me in the weeks that followed – my mother never said anything as clear as:

Your father is not coming back.

He is living with someone else.

He has another family over there.

It was simply something I came to understand, in the way children do, that things were no longer the same. One phase of your life is over, and suddenly you are a different person, even though you don't want to be, and had not been planning to change. The world rearranges itself around you, and all at once, you too are no longer the same. For a few bucks, my mother sold the baby clothes that she had been storing in a small box in the bedroom. She took the necklace that my father had given her on their wedding to the pawn-broker in town. She didn't take the wedding ring – that would follow some months later. Her visits to town were quick and efficient, wordless, without any ceremony or emotion. She had something to accomplish, another chore on her endless list of daily tasks that a single woman with a young child had.

You might say, So what? We needed money; we had to sell stuff – what was new? Still, it was different. There was a finality to those small acts that maybe the logic of adults – of clever, reasoned people like you – will interpret differently, will twist and reshape to form a kinder explanation. But a child always knows the truth, and in the end I was right. He never came back.

PERSEVERANCE AND RESILIENCE IN THE KOLA PENINSULA

Peter Frankopan

1936

—

MOROZ didn't need to look outside to know what the weather was like or if the sun had risen. He didn't care. As he pulled himself up to sit on the edge of his mattress, his muscles aching in the same places and the same ways they did every day, he breathed in slowly and watched the warm fumes form a cloud as he exhaled. He had given up counting the days long ago; if he had to guess, he might have said he'd been in Monchegorsk for just over three years. It wasn't that time stood still, rather that he felt he was living in a different dimension.

He pushed his toes into the paper he stuffed in his boots, a gesture against the ice and damp, before pulling them on and standing up. One of the others in the hut grunted as they ran dark, dirty fingernails through their hair in an attempt to dislodge the lice who inhabited the ramshackle wooden building along with the nine men. Moroz blinked as he opened the door and carefully walked down the steps on to the frost-covered ground before taking his usual place in the line-up, to be counted and checked by a wiry little man with a clipboard.

It was the same routine at the same time, every day since he had been there. Things did change. Sometimes, in the summer, the sun hardly set, so the five a.m. reveille took place in daylight; while in winter, the sun struggled to make it over the horizon before noon, then sagged back below it after a few short hours. The people changed too. No one who shared the cabin with Moroz had been there when he arrived. Most arrivals lasted a couple of months; some didn't even manage a few weeks.

Moroz had learned to tell how long a new inmate would take to break. The ones with hope in their eyes would be first to go, victims of their belief that things might get better, of their conviction that they would be allowed home one day. Some had heard that not fulfilling daily quotas in the nickel mine or that starting a fight could result in a transfer to the Kresty Prison in Leningrad and hoped that doing one or both might get them moved south.

Moroz would shrug when asked if it was true. He tried not to speak to anyone; he didn't want friends whose death would only hurt him even more. And he didn't want to be responsible either for raising the spirits of another man, or for being the one to dash them. He had no time, above all, for the wheeler-dealers, the career criminals or the sharp-witted, who thought they could thrive in the hell that was the most northerly reaches of the Soviet Union. He'd seen what had happened to them too, once each of their houses of cards had come tumbling down. If Moroz knew one thing, it was that if he was going to die up here in the bitterness of the icy Kola Peninsula, it would not be the elements that got him, nor the lead of a firing squad's volley.

As he was marched off to the mine, his ankle chained to the desperate figure in front and a man whose leg showed the unmistakable onset of gangrene behind him, he peered into the distance. He could see the outline of a small boat being prepared, likely for a fishing expedition; it wasn't big enough to be one of the new vessels whose job it was to 'protect the territorial integrity of the Union of Soviet Socialist Republics' – though only a madman or a Sámi or Nenets smuggler would be stupid enough to get anywhere close to where they could be caught and condemned to join the bedraggled, demoralised and almost useless band of those exiled to the north.

Moroz never thought much about what he was doing there. That was a sure way to bring on *toska*, that particular, overwhelming sense of longing and melancholy. He had seen men open their own wrists with tools they had managed to take back from the mine. He'd heard the groans they made as they bled to death. He had managed to find a way to block things out – to stop thinking. Perhaps the cold helped numb his mind as well as his hands, fingers, toes and everything else. To survive was all that mattered. He wasn't trying to survive because he wanted to get back home; in fact, there was part of him that didn't want to return. The idea of what he had left behind was painful enough. But he also knew that what had happened to him would have destroyed others around him – memory and reality were as bad as each other.

When the troubles had first started fifteen years earlier, he had been almost bemused. He'd been a signalman on the railway at Lozova, a few days' walk from where he'd been born, and would talk about the role he played in tying the ends of the empire together, whether he was wearing his uniform or not. He'd boorishly made his job sound more important and more difficult than it was. Lozova, he would tell his fellow drinkers in the *traktir* – the tavern by the station – was the beating heart of Russia, and it was his job to keep it pumping. As the evenings went on, he would repeat this with ever greater insistence until, in slow crescendo, his words were interrupted by the blue sound of a train passing through the town on its way from Kursk to the Sea of Azov.

Moroz knew something was happening early on because the trains started running without sticking to their timetable. And in the spring of 1917, when the snow began to thaw, drivers brought gossip that the Tsar had given up the throne and soon after that a new leadership had taken over the country. It was hard to know what was gossip and what was real, though Moroz understood that things were changing fast when Zossimov turned up one day and told everyone who would listen that he was no longer a soldier in the Imperial Army but had been appointed to oversee the redistribution of land.

That had not gone down well with everyone, as was clear when they found Zossimov hanging from a tree one evening, stripped to the waist. Moroz snapped to it and made for the city as quickly as he could. When he got there, he quickly learned that the best thing to do was not to hang around the markets or town squares trying to find out the latest news, but to look, dress and sound like one of the new leaders. He gathered up bundles of notices and orders handed down from on high and made himself useful, and visible. Rather than taking part in the looting of shops and houses, he took to sitting in on the meetings that ran late into the night and often well past dawn, discussing in fevered voices how the revolution would spread, and how joyful it was that the workers had finally been awakened.

He soon got used to the way they spoke, memorising and then parroting words about class struggle and the terrors of capitalism, learning the names of those whose works enabled him to claim intellectual high ground – even though he knew next to nothing about them. He did not mention how proud he had been of his uniform from Lozova and his role in helping Tsarist Russia run to time; instead, he talked of exploitation and the suffering of the 'people', without going into detail about who these people were.

Infected by a combination of enthusiasm, self-aggrandisement and the realisation that alongside the mantras of equality were the realities of new hierarchies forming, Moroz had abandoned his characteristic apathy and became a zealot. Armed with a revolver and a Swedish-made black leather jacket, he had been dispatched into the countryside to seek out trouble-makers. For several years, he took pride in identifying them, even when he knew they did not exist. He learned quickly that making an example of those who were admired in their communities was a way to break the resolve of all. Doing so made him feel powerful; not once did he feel guilty about what he'd done, because Moroz knew this was not about 'justice' or 'fairness'. It was about sacrifice: and why worry or think about those who were being martyred for a lost cause? He performed an occasional riffling of faces through his mind, some guiltier than others, none worthy of what he'd done to them, but none worth mourning either.

Moroz had seen some horrible things and was responsible for many of them. Nothing had been as bad as Ukraine in the early 1930s. He had been to one house where three generations of a family had starved to death, more than twenty of them huddled together in a single room. Then there was the time he had ordered his men to murder the inhabitants of an entire village because he needed to believe they had been hoarding grain. He knew in truth that the harvest had failed because of locusts and that the targets set from above were designed to be impossible to meet. But he had said and done nothing.

When they finally came for him, Moroz shouted, kicked and screamed. It was a misunderstanding; he demanded to know who was in charge. Then, most desperate of all, he asked if they knew who he was. The OGPU, of course, knew who everyone was. After a night in the cell, when his ribs were broken, one hand crushed and several teeth lost, he stopped trying. He knew how this worked. It was not about what was fair or right. It was not about being sorry or trying to repent. It was just how it was.

He assumed he would be shot after confessing that he had collaborated with the Ukrainians. Instead, he had been put on a windowless wagon to Karelia, the northern province bordering Finland that stretches like an arm into the Arctic

Circle, crammed alongside forty, perhaps fifty others. Ten of those loaded with him didn't wake up when the train stopped at Monchegorsk, frozen solid or too weak to survive the journey.

Monchegorsk and Murmansk, a hundred miles further north, were going to play a crucial role in the war that would set the world free from capitalism. That was what the Camp Commandant pompously told the new arrivals when they were taken off the train and made to stand upright in the snow to be formally welcomed. Comrade Kirov, the most popular man in the Soviet Union at the time, had said the Kola Peninsula was the jewel in the Soviet crown, a 'severe, barren, useless wilderness' which had turned out to be 'the richest place on earth'. Its mineral wealth would propel the country and its industry into the future. It would be extracted by men with few skills, little experience and no advantages, other than the fact that they had been categorised as being part of an infinitely numerous body of labour, and therefore expendable.

Because most had been classified as criminals, regardless of whether they had done something wrong, or, like Moroz, because time had simply caught up with them, there was no point bothering to look after them. There was a never-ending supply of men who could be rounded up and dispatched north whenever they were needed. They were put in rows of huts which had gaps in the floorboards, broken windows, beds with no mattresses and, instead of blankets, towels that had once belonged to the Black Sea fleet.

Moroz understood his lot. That made it easier for him to accept it. He recognised that the decision to leave trees standing in the centre of Monchegorsk and thus provide shelter from the wind was done to improve the lives of the officials – and that the reason trees had been cut down along the routes to and around the mines was to remind the condemned that they had earned their suffering. So much for being equal: even here, it was all about hierarchies.

Moroz had never been an extrovert and had never sought out the company of others, even in the old days. He had never settled down, found someone he enjoyed talking to into the small hours, never thought that he might like to have children of his own. He had always been a man who adapted to his surroundings, who looked for the course of least resistance, someone who thought hard about how to survive. None of this made him a good man. But living each day, each hour and each minute at a time gave him a certain strength. It helps to be numb if you think there is nothing to lose, and nothing to gain.

Moroz looked down, picked up his hammer and walked slowly through the mouth of the mine. One more day; one more day.

NO TIME TO WRITE
Yan Ge

I DECIDED to write a story to explain why I literally have no time to write. I think it's important to make official my no-time status so it can be comprehended, interpreted and remembered.

First of all, of course, time is an invented notion. It was introduced by the Power System so that we ordinary people could regulate our destructive primitive urges and find meaning on a day-to-day basis. Nonetheless, it's fake. So when I say I have no time to write, I neither have nor haven't time. In other words, time is not an order I choose to submit myself to. Or I question the very notion of order. Because if we consider ourselves as particles in the universe, we must acknowledge that the universe exists only in chaos. As explained in the second law of thermodynamics, our universe is a system where randomness is bound to increase. Any attempt to erase randomness and to create order is ultimately futile.

So when I am typing up these words on my laptop, I'm fundamentally a nameless object floating in the lightless universe. And my laptop, too, is another insubstantial object whose trajectory happens to be brushing against mine at this particular moment. And very soon, our collaborative effort towards generating order will be disrupted by the formidable power of randomness. And then we will be forced apart, orbiting, moving and brushing against other objects respectively.

This is why my writing will and has to stop. It is not because of the lack of time or any elaborate personal decision. It has to happen because of randomness.

I worship randomness.

✛

Some less interesting facts:

I was born in Singapore in 1982 to Irish parents. We moved to Hong Kong when I was just six weeks old because my father was needed there for a big merger. My younger brother was born three years later. When I was eight, my family moved to Shanghai where my father built the branch office of the company he worked for from scratch. I spent the majority of my adolescence in China before my family moved back to Ireland in 1999, when my father was asked to step down from the Shanghai office. I attended Trinity College in Dublin, studied Linguistics and Philosophy as an undergraduate and Post-Colonial Theory for my Masters. After graduation, I taught in a language school for four years and dated two East Asian girls. In 2008, when the language school had to cut back on its staff, I travelled back to Asia myself, freelancing and backpacking in Cambodia and Thailand. Then, this September, I returned to Dublin to my parents' house in Castleknock, and have been staying with them ever since.

Like everyone else, I'm troubled with my life but cannot really pin down my problems. I was once accused of being self-absorbed. Another girl I used to go out with told me this. 'You think you're a woman,' she said. 'But no, you are just a man trapped in a woman's body and horrendously straight. Cliona, you are shifting your sexual identity at your own convenience – so you can slip in and out of relationships. It's ridiculous and . . . exhausting.' She closed her eyes and tears escaped, sliding down along her cheeks and then vanishing beneath her brittle chin.

It was sad, and to an extent moving. But she was wrong. My biggest problem is I'm neither a man trapped in a woman's body nor do I have trouble committing to my sexual identity. My biggest problem is I don't believe in any of these preconceptions. Man/woman. A stable and non-fluid relationship. Gender identity. Cultural identity. And, to add to this list, time.

My father says I'm too smart for my own good. My mother says I'm just an ungrateful little brat.

'Won't you just get your bloody life together, Cliona?' she says, usually when she sees me in the kitchen, looking for food. 'Just get out of the house and get a life, for Christ's sake.'

'She has just come back, Fiona,' my father speaks up.

'From a bloody five-year-long holiday!'

My mother swears a lot at home. It is quite unusual considering she is a well-educated, middle-class woman whose life has been nothing but comfortable. She is all right when there are other people around, but if she is just with us, the poor woman can't help but spew out streams of obscenities. My father says it's just her way of releasing energy. 'We all need to find a way to let it out,' as he puts it.

I understand. Years of relocating and dislocating have injured each one of us in this family. Everyone except my little brother Ian. Ian lives in Porto with his girlfriend Sara and is as happy as a goldfish.

✧

In response to my mother's accusation, I'm actually trying to get my bloody life together. It is one of the reasons I want to write.   73

It happened in Chiang Mai, just a few weeks before I returned to Ireland. It was near dusk and I was sitting on the rooftop terrace of Sunset Lodge with Mama Mei, me drinking a bottle of Beer Lao, her smoking. It was my favourite time of day, when the temperature had finally cooled down and the city below had gone quiet. The nuns in the nearby convent were chanting some Buddhist sutra while pigeons circled in the coral-purple sky, aimlessly.

'Doesn't this feel extremely repetitive, so repetitive that it's almost, like, eternal?' I said to Mama Mei.

'Oh, not now, Cliona, not another round of your philosophising. It's been a long day for me.' She shook her head and took a drag.

'Fine.' I shrugged. 'I'm just saying.'

'Although I do like what you said the other day about the brushes,' she said.

'Not brushes. I was saying we don't really engage, we are just brushing against each other. It's all superficial,' I corrected her.

'Yes, yes.' She nodded with a smile. 'So you and Junjun are over?'

I shrugged again.

'What was wrong? She is a very nice girl,' she said. 'And you too.'

I drank a mouthful of beer. 'She wouldn't like to be called "a very nice girl". She'd probably say *nice* is a stigma for women and go on for hours – but no, nothing is wrong. It's just not working any more. Have you ever had this feeling, that we can't really be with another person even when we are physically with them? We're essentially dealing with ourselves all the time. And it's all repetitive. It haunts me, this idea that I'm just an object and she's a distorting mirror through which I increasingly see all the absurdity in myself . . .'

'You're thinking too much,' Mama Mei said.

'That's true,' I agreed. 'There is too much going on here. It's like the bus to Bangkok.' I pointed at my head.

Mama Mei laughed. 'You have too much energy in you,' she said, 'thoughts, ideas, memories . . . You have to let go of them. It's important to forget. Forgetting is a gift.'

'I know.' I sighed. 'Memory is the perpetual curse. Such a drag. It is colossal, ambiguous and changeable. I think about the past a lot. And every time I think of it, I essentially create a new version of it. It's an endless loop. A panopticon. I'm just trapped—'

'Why don't you write it all down?' Mama Mei interrupted me. 'You know, just like I keep a book for the Lodge. Who checks in when. Who drinks how much beer. I write everything down so I don't need to remember it all. On paper, out of head.'

'On paper, out of head,' I repeated.

'Exactly. Now, if you excuse me, I need to go get dinner. Do you need another beer?' She finished her cigarette, stood up and went down to the kitchen.

It was the end of August, the tourists were fleeing Thailand and people in Ireland began to realise the summer was over. 'Your mother wonders if you will be home for Christmas,' my father wrote in his email and said he'd love to book the ticket home for me.

It was the first time this offer had come up since I was fired from the language school for dating students and, that same night, told my parents I was gay. I flew back to Dublin. My father came to pick me up at the airport. 'Welcome home, Cliona,' he said with a broad smile as he took my luggage.

'How is Mam?' I said.

'She's cooking you a full Irish at home. We're both very glad you're back,' he said.

Ever since, I've been living at my parents' house. My sole mission is to write, to go down into my memories like a miner, get my hands dirty and get the nasties out. I stare at my computer screen and type down words, sentences, paragraphs. Things that happened. My opinions about the world. Terms, explanations, distinctions. And then I realise: I am actually not able to write.

One of the reasons could be Gemma. It had always been like this since we were in secondary school. Gemma wrote poetry. I replied with broken sentences.

The last time I met her was in Paris. I had just handed in my thesis for the postgraduate programme and I flew there on a fifteen-euro Ryanair ticket.

I stayed in this miniature hotel room not far away from the Sorbonne and texted to tell her I was there. For four days she didn't show up, saying she was busy with her deadline. Every day, I walked up and down Boulevard Saint-Michel for hours in the whooshing February wind. I remembered she'd mentioned once she got the bus from somewhere on Boulevard Saint-Michel to go to the university and I was hoping I would bump into her somehow. It didn't happen.

The fifth day she emerged. After 'pulling two all-nighters in a row' she looked as glamorous as a unicorn. 'Hi, Cliona.' She smiled when she saw me and reached out her arms. I walked up and hugged her. She was soft and smelled like fresh apricots.

'How's life?' she said.

'Not bad,' I said.

'And how's Fiona and Anthony? How's Ian?' she asked.

'They're all good,' I assured her.

We then stopped talking. It was very cold. I looked at the top of my boots.

'Burgers?' she suggested.

'Sure.' I nodded.

Gemma was obsessed with American fast food when we lived in Shanghai. She'd usually skip dinner at home and go to McDonald's with me. She could eat five spicy chicken burgers in a row, no problem.

That night in Paris we went to a Burger King near Luxembourg Gardens where we ate six double cheeseburgers and countless chips. Afterward, we walked across the road to a McDonald's and bagged ten discounted chocolate croissants to go. We shared the croissants as she walked me back to my hotel.

'This could be Shanghai,' I said.

'Shanghai forever,' she said in a singsong voice, as if we were in a TV commercial.

We were both hiccuping when we arrived outside my hotel. It was numbingly cold so I asked her if she wanted to go up.

'Sure. I think I need to puke,' she said. 'You do have a bathroom in your room, right?'

'Yes,' I said. We went upstairs. I pointed her to the bathroom and gave her a fresh towel. And then I sat on the bed, listening to her gagging loudly behind the door. It sounded like she was throwing up a baby.

She'd had bulimia for years. I thought she probably still did. Having missed it for quite a few years, I was slightly nauseated by the noise.

Eventually she came out. She looked very pale and sat down on the armchair.

'Can I have some water?' she asked.

I poured a glass and gave it to her.

She drank. 'Believe it or not, I haven't done this for ages.'

She started to sob. Her face was in her hands and she said: 'Why are you here?'

'Well.' I felt my throat was excessively dry. 'I miss you, I miss us.'

She snorted out half a laugh and raised her head. 'It's just nostalgia, isn't it? Last June, I had an abortion and I thought about you a lot, the way you always talk about those big deep ideas, your scepticism and the way you said, after we slept together for the first time, that you wished you were never born and the things about your parents . . .'

I wanted to tell her about the fight I had with my father before this trip but instead I walked towards her, knelt down in front of her and started to unbutton her jeans.

'What are you doing?' she said.

'It's OK,' I said, holding her hand. I pushed my face in between her legs.

'Are you mad?' She kicked me away. 'Oh my god, you're so self-absorbed!'

I sat on the floor and she continued. 'I really wanted to be nice to you. I told James I didn't want to see you but he said I should go. How stupid of me to listen to him, to think you might have changed!'

'Who is James?' I said.

'He is my fiancé,' she said. 'He is in my present and will be in my future. And what happened between us was all in the past. There is no point holding on to the past. It has nothing to do with the present. It's just in your head. And it's in everybody's best interest if you just keep it in your head.'

✧

She was wrong. Gemma Wong-Laurent is an extremely bright young woman but she was totally wrong on this. The past has everything to do with the present. In fact, the past and the present are a set of interdependent notions. The past only establishes itself as the past of the present. And the present needs to take the past as its reference so it can be defined. We can only conclude today is the present if we set yesterday as the past, or this minute the present if the minute just gone is the past. In other words, the past and the present are inseparable. The line between them is only relative and always in flux.

After Paris, I posted Gemma the full three volumes of *Time and Narrative* by Paul Ricœur, along with a ten-page introduction drafted by myself. As a result, I missed the job interview my father set up for me and ended up working in a language school near Parnell Square. To which my mother commented: 'I told you to stay away from the Laurents. They are a damned bunch.'

Blaming Gemma or not, the situation is that I am just not able to write. I find everything dubious, bland and problematic. In order to feel inspired I read as much as I can, day and night, awake or half-asleep. Propelled by an extraordinary sense of urgency I read about the origins of tribes, the structures of hegemony, the anatomy of animal bodies, etc.

It is when my mother finds out I'd been forcing myself to get sick four times a day that she decides we need to get help. After consulting old colleagues, my father contacts a reputable psychoanalysis institute in Malahide. He drives me there for an interview.

A short-haired woman in her forties leads me into a room. Her handshake is affirmative, her smile alluring. She asks me my name, date of birth and my history of allergies. She chats with me for about forty minutes in a soft and sympathetic voice. Two days later she phones me, telling me my application is accepted. I need to go in on Tuesday at two p.m.

On Tuesday, my father drives me to the institute and I am directed to the same room. Behind the door, on the same chair across the room, is seated not the woman but a fifty-something man.

'Hello, Cliona. My name is Noel. Come in and sit.' He nods at me.

I am not sure if they changed to a different doctor or I misremembered my last meeting. I walk over and sit down, put my handbag on the floor.

'Hi, Noel,' I greet him.

'We had a meeting on Friday, deciding who would be the most suitable person to work with you.' He speaks very slowly, as if somebody is typing in his stomach and the voice comes out from his mouth. 'We think I might be the best person and I am happy to be here, to help you.'

'Thank you.'

'Good. So, let's start. First, can you tell me why you are here?' he asks me.

I explain the reasons.

'I see. Can you tell me a little bit about your relationship with your parents? How's it like with your mother, and with your father?'

I answer the questions.

'OK. Then let's talk about your father first. Tell me more about him. What does he do? What's he like?'

I speak for a while, gesturing with my hands and laughing the odd time.

Noel waits until I finish and he says: 'I've noticed one thing since you came in, Cliona. You withdraw your feelings. Every time that you're about to get emotional, you pull back. You analyse and ridicule yourself. Why do you do it?'

It's a tough question. I think about it and suggest a few possibilities.

'I don't know the answers,' he says. 'I'm just asking the questions. Now let's continue. Do you want to talk a bit more about what happened in Shanghai, between you and your father?'

I speak. This time I pay more attention to the emotional flow. I poise myself and pace through.

'You are kind,' he says. 'Another person would have been very angry. Or at least would have let him know how she felt.'

I respond to his comments.

'I'm not the judge here. If you think your decision is right then it is the right one for you,' he says. 'If I might point out, it's important for us to cry and to feel angry. There is no shame in it. Happiness, sadness, jealousy, anger, they are all discharges of our body. Is earwax better than snot?'

I lift up the corners of my mouth for a smile.

He looks at the wall behind me and says: 'I'm afraid our session is about to finish. Now, Cliona, I want to ask you for one more thing. When you go back, can you write down what happened today? What you said to me, can you write it down? You don't have to show it to anyone. Just write, type it up on your computer and delete it afterwards. But write first.'

'I'll try,' I say.

I leave the institute and walk to the Costa next to Malahide Castle to meet my father. He is reading the *Independent* and puts down the paper when he sees me.

'How did it go?' he asks.

'It went well,' I say.

He folds up the newspaper, leaves it on the chair and picks up his coat. We walk towards the exit. He places his hand on my lower back briefly and says: 'I'm very proud of you.'

✢

What is so significant about writing? Why is there this omnipresent and ceaseless craving to write, as if it were a ritual? Let's go back to the notion of randomness and our hopeless struggle against it as a species. Randomness is the fundamental law of the universe and it compels us to forget. It is our nature to forget and it's also in our nature to resist it. To write does not facilitate forgetting. Rather, it's the ultimate manifestation of remembering. To concretise it with language, to engrave it on stone, to encapsulate it in books, to pass it on and make it eternal.

It sounds incredibly appealing. But still, I find myself feeling sceptical about any kind of order. Because it turns everything into signifiers and draws power to the centre. All order is a system for rule. By whom? I don't know. I will stay vigilant and discover the answer.

I have trouble falling asleep and when I finally do I have trouble staying asleep. As a result, I'm awake all the time. It prolongs the days and makes life more intolerable. In order to get myself going, I eat a lot.

I go to the kitchen in the middle of the night and devour whatever we have in the fridge. One morning, my mother gets up and finds no bread, no milk, no cereal – no nothing. She becomes extremely upset, especially since she usually wakes up with low blood sugar.

'Can't you just leave something for me, for Christ's sake?' she bellows. 'I need to eat right now! Jesus, I can't breathe!'

Her face turns pale, lips purple. She falls down into an armchair and pants with her mouth open. 'Anthony!' She calls my father. 'Anthony! Anto!'

Nobody answers. It seems my father is not in the house.

'Let me find something for you. I'm sure we have something somewhere.' I open the cupboards and start searching. Finally, behind the gas meter, I find a half-finished Mars bar. I smell it.

'Do you want to have this? I'll go to the shop now to get you some breakfast. But have this for now.' I hand her the bar.

She looks at it and eats. The packaging rustles off like snakeskin.

'Do you want to have some water?' I ask her.

She nods. I give her some water before I grab the car key to get groceries.

Who hid the Mars bar behind the gas meter? I wonder as I start the engine.

The engine starts. I reverse my mother's red Volvo slowly out of the driveway.

Later, I call my brother Ian. He answers immediately.

'Hello *Jiejie*, how's life?' His voice is bright and almost too loud. And he calls me *Jiejie* as always, Chinese for older sister.

'Not bad. And you?' I say.

'Excellent. Couldn't be better,' he replies.

'Guess what I found behind the gas meter this morning.'

'The gas meter?' He pauses for a while before he laughs out loud. 'Don't tell me the Mars bar is still there!'

'Yep. And it saved Mam's life,' I tell him.

'She's welcome,' he says.

'How are you doing?' he asks me.

'I am trying to write but it isn't working,' I say. 'They're sending me to a therapist.'

'How generous,' he replies.

We change the subject. He tells me Sara is settling into her second trimester. They are making a trip to Naples next month.

'Come to join us,' he suggests. 'It'd be lovely for you to meet Sara. And trust me, you'll feel so much better when you get out of that house.'

'I'm afraid I can't,' I say. 'The situation is not great here with Mam and Dad. I think Dad is doing his thing again and that's why Mam wanted me to come back.'

He doesn't speak for a while. He sighs. 'Why can't they just get a divorce?'

'You know what Mam is like,' I say.

'Of course I do, the two of you.'

'What do you mean?' I say.

He laughs as if I'd told a joke. 'I need to go now,' he says. 'It'd be nice to see you at some point.'

'It would be,' I say.

'*Zaijian, Jiejie*,' he says.

My mother discusses my situation over dinner.

She asks my father: 'I think Cliona is getting worse. Do you think the therapy really works? That place is very good according to people from your work, no?'

'It's the best,' my father says. 'I think she enjoys the therapy.'

'Do you?' She turns to me. 'Do you like the therapy, Cliona, have you been taking the pills the doctor gave you?'

'He didn't give me a prescription. He said my situation was only mild.' I pierce a rocket leaf with my fork.

'Do you hear that, Anto?' she asks my father again. 'Does she look mild to you?'

'Maybe.' My father nods. 'We should leave this to the professionals.'

'God bless us.' She sighs.

'God bless,' I echo as I halve a cherry tomato, skewer it with a piece of spinach, and then a slice of cucumber.

My mother is so lucky that she believes in God. I'm envious of her ability to find a place to rest, a corner to turn to. And my biggest problem, as far as I can see, is that I don't believe in anything. Our lives exist on the constant movement of atoms and subatomic particles. And our thoughts are trapped within the structures of language. I'm baffled both by the profundity of the former and the limitations of the latter. I feel nauseous whenever thinking about the distance between them. To a certain extent, everybody in my life, the ones I deeply love, and the ones I pass by on the street, is the same. We are objects in this universe, confined by our epistemological limits. We brush against each other for exceedingly short moments and we drift apart. We will never be able to understand ourselves, let alone each other. I bow down to the sublimity of the impossible.

And this is exactly why I cannot write. I sit alone in my bedroom, staring at the screen of my laptop, hands on the keyboard, motionless. I think of the warm damp summer nights in Shanghai when my mother cried by herself like a beast and my brother Ian would sneak into my bedroom in his pyjamas and say: '*Wo haipa, Jiejie.*' I'd bring him into my bed and say: 'It's going to be OK.'

From downstairs I can hear my mother sobbing. She cries for so long that the rhythm of her crying begins to change, like the tide receding into the sea. Another day is over. And my father has left the house.

I realise that I'm looking forward to seeing Noel on Tuesday.

NEAR THE FAR SIDE OF THE WORLD

Lawrence Osborne

JUST before midday, on the road to Mandalgovi, Jalsa Soronzonbold had his driver pull over their Land Cruiser and told his guest, a solitary Englishman who had just arrived from Hong Kong, that they were going to stop for a picnic on the summit of a hill not far from the road. Chittleborough, a retired banker of about sixty, agreed to a pause after a drive of six hours. To the Mongol's eye he was louchely elegant, enigmatic. He wore a stylish Motoluxe teddy bear coat of pale grey mohair and there was something inscrutable and subtly domineering about him, even though his manners were impeccably subdued. He coughed into his hand, though, and his face had a feverish sheen. He had booked Jalsa's New World Lodge all for himself with a down payment of $8,000. He had told the owner that he wished to go on a snow leopard safari with Jalsa himself as his guide. He wanted to see the world's most elusive animal before he died. It was a modest request.

'Is he dying, then?' Jalsa had thought at the time, and he thought it again now.

It was a blue morning late in October. The Mongol's eye went once more over the Motoluxe coat and the fine jodhpur boots with their Coimbra patina. The visitor certainly had money, whether he was dying or not. But what if he really was on the way out? Although Jalsa had grown up in New Jersey, a child of illiterate Kalmyk immigrants, he had not lost the beliefs of his ancestors. He determined to take the man to a shaman that same day.

'Do you always stop here?' the Englishman asked, as they climbed up a hill towards a picnic table which the drivers had set up. There was a spread of caviar and blinis and a few bottles of whisky which Jalsa had won while playing the tables in Las Vegas. He was a construction millionaire back in the States, a high roller at the casinos in his spare time. When he lost big, the grateful casinos gave him expensive bottles.

'I never know if it's the same hill. But yes.'

'Do you mind if we pause a bit?'

They were out of breath as they stood in the grass, and yet the horizons inspired them. The Englishman shielded his eyes and saw how cleanly the steppes ran to the earth's edge. Ravines and long ridges filled with shadows where the grass must be about to die as winter came. On a hill nearby an *ovoo* of piled whitewashed stones stood in the sun, its prayer flags fluttering around it.

For a moment, as Jalsa looked the stranger over, he had a curious passing thought: Chittleborough's beard, flecked with grey and quite long, was not entirely real. It might have been a transplant of some kind. His nose dripped with unusual sweat. Soon, however, the first bottle had been opened and they were seated in pop-up canvas chairs as their pulses slowed. Jalsa put on his shades and set his feet on a little stool which they always brought for him. He ordered the two cans of chilled caviar to be opened.

'I'm curious about you, James,' he said. 'Most people come here to forget and heal. But is that you?'

'Not really. I just felt like being in motion. I felt like driving for a long time. I suppose it's a bit foolish, but I thought I needed a last hurrah.'

'A last hurrah?'

'Well, so to speak.'

'What about a last drink?'

The Englishman crossed his boots and when he had come to the end of his cigarette he carefully disposed of the butt in a saucer instead of tossing it to the wind. Jalsa appreciated the little gesture. He leaned over and poured the first glass of the new bottle. Along the road below the two vans sat idle by the verge, shining like black beetles taking a nap. Around them was only the golden grass, bright as an ocean.

'Did you know,' he said to Chittleborough, 'my father never saw the land of his ancestors even once? He was born in the Crimea and then emigrated to the United States. The world is a monstrous place.'

But he was smiling. He went on to explain that he had built his desert lodge in the Gobi entirely by himself using shamanistic rituals and traditional methods. There were no metal nails.

'It's my monument,' he said. 'Do you have a monument, Adrian?'

'I can't say I do, unfortunately. It's a shame, I suppose you could say—'

'Well, you have time.'

'In fact,' Chittleborough said, 'that's the one thing I don't have.'

'You have to make the time. These things take years to build.'

Chittleborough merely scanned the steppe and the flapping Buddhist flags, as if wanting to end the conversation there. He coughed for a moment and raised his hand to cover his mouth.

When they came down from the hill it was two o'clock. They turned on some Johnny Cash and rolled down the windows. Two hours later they finally passed through Mandalgovi, nestled under rock cliffs. It was windblown, grimly tenacious, hanging on by shredded fingernails.

Impoverished white *gers* stood on dusty slopes with their chimneys smoking, the yards surrounded by low walls. It was the gateway to the desert. By dusk they had reached Dalanzadgad, a frontier town where their Cruiser was going to be serviced for the onward voyage. The place was already plunged in darkness. Packs of white dogs raced through it unhindered and suddenly delirious. Dusk, however, was offset by arc-lamps hung on construction cranes and by the temple-like glare of gas stations emblazoned with the single Cyrillic word *Petrovis*. At the end of Soviet boulevards the mountains rose up under bursts of clouds lit by the sunset; along them, the prefab warehouses glistened with what looked like frost.

While they waited for the car to be refitted, Jalsa suggested they go to a karaoke bar and waste an hour some-where warmer. It was called the Marco Polo II, a lounge set next to a parking lot filled with drifts of sand. When they arrived, Jalsa and Chittleborough went in alone, past half-gone miners propped in darkness at the bar and Chinese prospec-tors who had driven in from the desert for a night away from their boredom and their bauxite mines. There was a jukebox playing Russian hits and some local toughs were shooting pool at the far end. They were glad of the gloom. Jalsa offered the visitor a shot, took off his fur hat and gloves and laid them on the bar. Between songs they could hear the windows soughing. They toasted Chittleborough's arrival and Jalsa decided on a whim to call him 'brother', a term reserved for the few.

'Meanwhile,' he said, 'I'm going to have to fix this music.'

Getting up, he strode to the jukebox. In his steel-capped cowboy boots and New York shirt he cowed the pool players into acquiescence. Soon, the steely strains of 'Apache' met their ears and they stopped for a moment to watch the Mongol exile from New Jersey lope back to his stool. The barman came over and said that 'Apache' was his favourite song on the box, a true Mongolian classic.

'My father loved that song,' Jalsa said to Chittleborough. 'But he never saw Mongolia and he never learned to read. That's how it is.'

'He would be proud of you now.'

They clacked glasses. Chittleborough talked a bit more about himself. He had been a high roller of sorts back in his day. He had made his millions, invested them wisely and then, in his way, grown bored of them. He lived in Hong Kong and London but no longer cared which. He owned a small mansion on The Peak in Hong Kong and spent his days managing distant charities. He was divorced; his grown up children lived in the States and seemed to despise him. It was a common fate of driven men. What compensations, then, did boundless wealth offer? All the world's cities, he explained, were becoming indistinguishable from each other. What he craved most these days was an open road, but they were increasingly few and far between. Then one day he had seen the website for the New World and he had read that at Mongolia's foremost eco-resort one could ride horses to the horizon and sleep in a tent. The roads there were so wild that no one could honestly call them roads.

Jalsa was about to bring up the delicate subject of shamans, but before he could do so Chittleborough brought it up himself. He had seen flyers for telephone shamans slipped under his door at the Ulaanbaatar Shangri-La the night before. Could they really foretell the future?

'I believe they can,' Jalsa confessed, 'but the news is never good. I do believe everything they say, though.'

'Everything?'

'I'll take you to one tonight if you like. There are several in Dalanzadgad. Are you sure about it?'

'I've heard they are great mindreaders. I need it.'

Chittleborough paid for the shots and they went back outside into the whirling cement dust. Jalsa called ahead to a shaman who worked on the outskirts of the town, a woman he knew quite well, and they drove there without saying a word.

The stars had now come out and, once they had driven beyond the perimeter of the town, the light was all in the sky. At the edge of the desert they came to a cinderblock shack with prayer flags around it flapping in the wind and the soft sound of a television coming from the interior. They knocked and an old woman in tracksuit bottoms and an outer coat pegged with animal furs opened it. She was prepared for them and already heating milk. Behind her, a fire with coals warmed the room to the temperature of a sauna. The price was thirty dollars.

The woman had them sit and she greeted Jalsa as if she knew him well. They talked while Chittleborough sat on his haunches taking in the rags spattered with sour milk on the walls and the pelts hanging from nails. Desert foxes or rats and rabbits. A tattered calendar lay on the floor. Jalsa finally turned to him.

'She wants you to mark your birthdate on this calendar.'

When he did so, she said to Jalsa, 'Birthdate 1960. Element water – picky rat.'

'How can a rat be picky?' Chittleborough objected.

'It's in the zodiac.'

Then the ceremony began. She donned a headdress with feathers and a leather mask, drank some milk mixed with vodka and began beating a small drum with moons painted on the skin. Soon she was swaying.

It went on for fifteen minutes. Then she threw a bowl of her milk onto the pelts on the wall and turned again to Jalsa. He translated for Chittleborough. The spirits wanted to know what the Englishman was doing in their land. Why had he come there and what did he want? Why was he wearing black, a cursed colour? Did he not like milk?

Chittleborough calmly answered that he had come to see snow leopards and to visit a shaman, which he was now doing, and that most of his clothes were black. He liked milk. The shaman herself then turned and threw yet more milk over him and then reached out and laid her hand on top of his head. The spirits were curious about him and they could see everything, past and future. Drenched in sour milk, Chittleborough asked the spirits what lay in store for him over the next few days.

'He will sleep for two days,' the shaman said to Jalsa. 'He will wake up on the third day.'

'And beyond that?'

She spoke very quietly so that the foreigner would not be suspicious.

'He is sick. The spirits say he has a terminal cancer. Did he not tell you? Otherwise they say he will be prosperous.'

'It's what you say to everyone.'

'In his case, it's a strong message. He will be prosperous but he will die. It's up to you if you want to tell him.'

They went outside for a smoke afterwards and Chittleborough said that he had enjoyed the ritual. But what had the shaman said about his future?

'She said you'll live to be a hundred and make another fortune.'

'Really? That's a very nice message from the spirit world for thirty dollars. But what do the spirits have against the colour black?'

'It's an unlucky colour here. I should have told you before you came.'

In reality, Jalsa was filled with a cool dread. He did believe what the spirits said, for all his American upbringing, and had he not already intuited that the Englishman was mortally sick?

Back at the gas station the Cruiser was ready and they continued their journey over open desert. Five miles beyond the little airport the surfaced road expired. They turned on the jeep's big roof lights as they drove. Low *gers* lay in the light, surrounded by thorn fences and tamarisks, and around them shone ancient chalk covered by feather grass and winterfat.

As the thermometer dropped, they set their teeth and waited for the lights of New World to appear out of the nothingness, like those of a Christmas play on a night of snow. Jalsa called ahead to the staff, and as they pulled up to the resort four boys in nomad dress stood at the head of a path lit by toadstool lamps. Since Chittleborough had paid handsomely for his privacy, they were the only arrivals that week.

Chittleborough's bags were carried on shoulders to his *ger*. At a glance, he thought there were maybe two dozen of these felt tents on stone foundations. Their doors opened onto the desert. A kind of clubhouse sat in the middle of it, with curved and painted eaves. 'The end of all roads,' he thought with satisfaction. The clubhouse turned out to be a whisky bar stocked with Vegas trifles. It had an open fire and was filled with Gobi dinosaur teeth. He had intended it to evoke a cosy hotel in the Highlands. Even the rafters had been built with his own bare hands.

Above the resort a tumulus rose to a plateau of volcanic rock. It was covered with prehistoric tombs marked by low piles of rocks which had slumbered there for three thousand years. On their smoothed surfaces were carved pictographs of archers and gazelles, sun and moons. Chittleborough lingered there for a while before dinner, marvelling at these images. Then he went back down to the steps of the clubhouse on his way to his accommodation. The wind had already chilled his ears to numbness.

Inside, the staff were dancing by themselves, thinking no one could hear them. Teenage students from Ulaanbaatar. The bar didn't open officially for another hour and they had it all to themselves. He sat on the steps and felt a great delight. The road by which they had come was just a scratch mark on the surface of the icy desert. Here a cluster of wild horses stood in the moonlight flicking their tails. He sat and reflected on his long day, which, after all, had begun in Hong Kong. Many things had happened since his pre-dawn breakfast overlooking the South China Sea. A shaman had told him that he would make another fortune and that he was a fool for wearing black. Shaking his head and chuckling, he made his way down to his *ger* and ran a long lukewarm shower, then lay on the bed covered with nomad quilts. The staff came in every four hours to re-fuel the stove whose metal chimney kept the tent warm, and they were there then. Two boys carrying a brazier and tongs. After they had left, he stretched out and enjoyed the suffocating heat. He had forgotten about dinner and simply fell asleep.

In the dining room, meanwhile, Jalsa sat alone with a bottle that he had also won in Las Vegas. He opened it morosely and began to drink. By ten, he thought that the Englishman had maybe forgotten about dinner altogether and sent a boy down to check up on him. Sure enough, the boy reported back, the visitor was fast asleep. So asleep that nothing could wake him. 'Then let him sleep,' Jalsa said, and ate his *khorkhog* alone. From the middle of the mutton he picked up the hot stone and rubbed his hands in sheep fat. His mood had darkened. So the foreigner had fallen asleep after all, though in the circumstances it was understandable. Perhaps the road had exhausted him.

When he returned to his own *ger*, he lit incense and recited prayers to Buddha before finding sleep himself. That night, however, his dreams were not graced by the compassion of Buddha. Instead, he found himself walking the plain in a heavy snow that did not melt on his eyelashes. In the middle of the desolate plain he met the shaman again, who was squatting by a small fire and waiting for him. Though they spoke, their mouths did not open. He asked her if the spirits were watching over the Englishman and she said that during the night the stranger had disappeared from view. 'Look,' she said, pointing to footprints in the snow that trailed off into the mist. He had gone that way alone, taking his cancer with him. 'Like the picky rat,' she said, 'that he is.'

When Jalsa woke, the first thing he heard was a light snow pattering on the roof of the *ger*. On his cell phone he called the kitchen to bring him down his pu'er tea. He went outside to drink and before the boy left he asked him about the visitor. Had Chittleborough come up for an early breakfast?

'No one has seen him, sir.'

So he must be sleeping in late.

'Let the fire in his *ger* go cold and it will wake him up.'

Outside his *ger*'s hearth Jalsa sat on a folding chair and drank his tea as the plain around him turned white. After his dream he had been briefly woken by the howl of wolves, but as usual they had not come near the resort. He brooded over the strange Englishman. At last, the staff came to him and reported that Chittleborough was still asleep and that the chill of the *ger* had not roused him. He had by now been asleep for more than fourteen hours. Jalsa decided to go down and see for himself. When he got to Chittleborough's tent, however, his dread returned and he hesitated before entering. Not for nothing do the spirits send us dreams when they want to warn us. And inside the tent the Englishman lay on his side, breathing softly. His passport sat on the night table along with a blister pack of Ultracet painkillers. Jalsa looked over the unopened bags and felt a sly desire to rifle through them. But a guest was a guest. Even if, in the end, he had no idea who this stranger really was.

Chittleborough slept through the whole day and then into the evening. The staff gossiped about the Englishman who had not woken since he arrived. All through the night they stood guard over him, now periodically lighting the fire in his *ger* under new orders from the boss. The boys who made the fire in his room whispered that he was in a trance and would never wake up. Jalsa himself, sitting outside the *ger* during the night and listening to the far-off wolves, began to think that the shaman was far more powerful than even he had anticipated.

The following day the clouds had cleared. Stilled by snow, the plain shone like silver. Jalsa waited all day by the satellite phone, equivocating. Then, as the light finally faded and brilliant stars scattered across the sky, there was a stirring from inside Chittleborough's *ger* and the boy posted outside his door ran up to tell his boss.

Jalsa went down and opened the door himself. In the gloom he saw Chittleborough sitting up in bed and rubbing his eyes.

'I'm terribly sorry,' he said. 'I must be late for dinner. Did I oversleep? You should have woken me.'

'We tried, but we thought you needed a good rest.'

'What time is it?'

'Time for dinner, I'd say. Are you hungry?'

'I'll say. Starving. And I could use a drink.'

'Then get freshened up and I'll meet you in the clubhouse.'

It was an hour before Chittleborough appeared, his hair still wet and neatly combed, his beard oiled. The Englishman was now spruce, like a Victorian Arctic adventurer who has finally come home to hearth and home.

'I had the damnest sleep,' he said energetically, his eyes bright and wide. 'Many dreams – but now I can't remember them.'

'Maybe it's better.'

'About tomorrow – are we driving out to the mountain range to see the snow leopards?'

'Tomorrow?'

For a moment Jalsa was confused. Then he realised that Chittleborough had no idea that he had been sleeping for two days.

'Why, of course. It's a long drive though. I hope you can deal with it.'

'I've been sleeping solidly since I arrived. Tomorrow I'll be in tremendous shape. Don't worry. Why wouldn't I be able to deal with it?'

'In that case we'll get up at four a.m., if it's all right with you.'

'It's more than all right. I've never felt better.'

They drank a few brandies after dinner next to a roaring fire in their overcoats and fur hats. One of the boys came up and played his *morin khuur*. Jalsa could see the relief in his face that the foreigner had not remained in his trance. He showed Chittleborough his military survey map marked with the nomad tracks winding into the surrounding Gurvan Saikhan range. The Chinese border was only sixty miles to the south, a no-man's-land filled with Soviet military ruins. In this wilderness, they would find the leopards.

In the event, they rose earlier and left at four, just the two of them. They took with them a rifle, two binoculars, cameras, boxes of sandwiches, two traditional recurved bows with blunted arrows and a satellite phone. Before they left, Jalsa told his staff not to betray to Chittleborough that he had slept for two days. A man paying $8,000 had a right to his peace of mind, at least until he returned to the airport and discovered the truth. Then it wouldn't matter. There was no internet in the Gurvan Saikhan.

By first light they were alone on the steppe. In the distance, wild camels moved like caravels across the grassland and to the east; like something out of Ezekiel's dreams, a black tornado appeared for a while and then faded away. As the snow melted under a clear sun, the track which Jalsa already knew by heart became visible to the eye, reaching to the far horizon, a path carved into grass that nomads had used for centuries.

A hundred kilometres down it they stopped and drew out

the two bows Jalsa had brought with them. They took it in turns to shoot the arrows high into the air and let them thud into the weakened snow. The sun blinded the Englishman and he covered his eyes. As they walked over to retrieve the arrows, Chittleborough said that he felt rejuvenated in some indefinable way. This was what he had come looking for. Space and grass.

'And there was something I didn't tell you previously,' he added. 'Before I left Hong Kong my doctor diagnosed me with a rare cancer which is apparently difficult to treat. Therefore, this might well be my last trip anywhere on earth. Since I thought this might be the case, I decided to come here. I certainly don't regret it.'

'That is sad news, Adrian. I'm very sorry to hear it.'

But the Englishman didn't seem sad at all. As he picked up the arrows his expression was childishly happy.

'No, I feel marvellous, I have to admit. Shall we sit and have a sip of something?'

'You're asking a Mongol?'

By the jeep they laid out a blanket and drank from a flask with strips of beef jerky. A rainbow had appeared in place of the come-and-go tornado, and the snow had almost completely disappeared. Chittleborough talked about his plans for what could be a very short future, but without bitterness. Eventually, though, Jalsa asked him about his sleep. Had Chittleborough experienced something during it, an encounter of some kind?

'What kind of encounter?'

'I don't know. Sometimes we believe that we have a glimpse of death in a dream. Did you?'

But the Englishman's eyes were blank.

'I woke up very afraid, now that you mention it. But then I heard the fire and the wind and I was happy. Like I am now. I knew where I was.'

'I'm glad to hear it. We'll drive for ten hours today. And we probably won't see a snow leopard.'

'It's neither here nor there.'

'By the way,' Chittleborough added, 'did you hear the wolves last night?'

'Of course. But they only attack during rain. It's a known fact.'

'Ah, is that so?'

The Englishman looked confused for a moment but said nothing further. Indeed, they hardly spoke for the rest of the day, since everything that needed to be said had already been uttered. Inside the dry ravines of the Gurvan Saikhan they never saw a snow leopard. Even when Chittleborough had left the following day, Jalsa was unsure what to think about the long sleep of the visitor. He had meant to explain it to him when they got to Ulaanbaatar airport but to his surprise the Englishman said nothing about it. He glanced at his ticket, smiled, and got on the plane without a word.

At the Shangri-La Hotel that night Jalsa went on the internet and googled Adrian Chittleborough. The visitor didn't exist, however, not in that dimension anyway. The only Chittleborough he could find was a reputable tailor on Savile Row, maker of twill suits for gentlemen and mentioned frequently on the website Dashing Tweeds. How he wished now that he had discreetly opened his passport that night and found out his real name.

SO *THAT'S* WHAT YOU THINK A SOUL IS FOR

Katharine Kilalea

THERE were fluorescent lights in the consulting room. Flo lay down beneath the painting of a Renaissance-style woman reclining on a chaise with the words *it is the mind that makes the body* written above her in cursive script. The papery, blue curtains around the bed billowed as the obstetrician opened the door. How are you feeling? she said. But Flo's feeling was difficult to describe. Well, the obstetrician wanted to know – being, as doctors are, pragmatic about feelings – what does it feel *like*? Like a mobile phone, said Flo, on vibrate. Interesting, the obstetrician said, and who do you think is calling?

Can you tell that someone has no one inside them just by looking at them? The obstetrician apologised for the coldness of the consulting room, which was large and badly insulated, and for the coldness of her hands feeling downwards from Flo's belly button to her womb. Flo watched the probe rooting around the inner surfaces of her body, pushing her organs to one side. She didn't like the sight of herself: she was too bulbous, seen from within. Where previously there'd been a heartbeat – something pulsing – were just vague gelatinous shapes dissolving into each other, organs which, had the obstetrician not described them by their anatomical names, Flo would've been unable to recognise. There's nothing here, said the obstetrician, or if there is we can't see it any more.

Meanwhile, the vibrating continued. It was late January. Snow was falling over the city. A woman standing outside the hospital was talking on her phone. He was my best friend, she cried. Was she a doctor? People were wearing coats so the distinction between doctors and patients was problematic. A man describing treatment for his condition said, And what makes death any different? Flo waited ages for a taxi then finally one arrived. They drove three miles west and two miles south. She was coatless. Aren't you cold? the driver said, and she supposed she was. He lent her his coat to wear and she wore it. On the radio a coroner describing a mother and daughter who'd died in a fire said, We buried them in a single grave because their bodies were impossible to separate.

I know it's unfashionable to say such things, the obstetrician had said, but what about a metaphysical cure? So at seven a.m. the following morning Flo made her way to the address on the bottom of the invoice.

The obstetrician said that Flo's womb had become susceptible to – how had she put it? – *ordinary vibrations*, the kind that are always there, only you don't usually notice them. A womb shouldn't be too sensitive, she'd said. Indifference is the ideal state for a womb. Didn't Flo know that women fell pregnant the moment they stopped thinking about it? The best way to conceive a baby was not to conceive of it. It's true, Flo thought about the baby too much. The thought of the baby was toxic; it made her sick. Morning sickness, the obstetrician had said. Mourning sickness, Flo had heard.

The yoga instructor paused mid-sentence as Flo arrived and the group of students, bent forward, looked up in mutinous, uncomprehending resentment. The workshop was meant to restore the body's *natural vibrational state*, but for now they seemed to be doing a visualisation exercise, eyes closed, arms waving as if clearing the air in front of them. What's that in the water? the instructor was saying. It's kelp. And what's that swimming at the foot of the kelp? It's a flat fish. Now imagine I'm a kelp and you're some kind of flat fish lurking low in the water . . . The pose was unnatural. Flo's pelvis hurt. She'd assumed she'd become immune to the discomfort, or that they'd stop the pose and move on, but they kept it up for some time until, perhaps because of the pain, Flo's hips began to tremble. And the yoga must really have been working because now she felt it shifting, rippling from her hips into her chest, and then her throat, so that as the blood welled in her skull, making her face redden, her lips and eyes began to twitch.

Previously the vibrating had been bearable-ish, but now it was totally unbearable. Only of course it wasn't unbearable because Flo didn't die. Flo waited for the vibrating to subside – ten nine eight seven six five four – but it didn't go away. Someone was calling . . . Someone was calling . . . Maybe it was her father, always dialling her by mistake, repeatedly, so she'd hear his phone rubbing against the fabric of his jacket, or her Eurosceptic husband – Italy has so much gold it could walk away from the Euro tomorrow – or the obstetrician, or some deeper, more private, communication, from the baby perhaps – I haven't forgotten you, Flo – or the phone itself – I'm sorry I can't be who you want me to be.

The instructor said Ohmmm and Flo couldn't stop herself joining in. She opened her mouth to say something or make some noise to discharge the feeling, but when she opened her mouth she said, I don't know. Because although the idea of it disgusted her – you couldn't help imagining it, that piece of plastic moulded against those dappled inner walls – the inner phone seemed to Flo the expression of some inner good, something worth keeping hold of, like her *soul*, perhaps. Because that's what frightened her, her soul escaping

103

on a gust of breath. Oh, I don't know, Flo said again with a regretful sort of sigh, because she didn't want to overestimate the soul or put it on a pedestal, because of course nobody knows what happens in a soul . . . But still, she didn't like the idea of her soul feeling like a mobile phone.

The students didn't speak to each other during the class but afterwards they did. Look at me, one said, patting a round belly, I'm having a food baby. Me too, said another, putting on her shoes, I've been constipated for so long that there'll be a geyser one day. On another day, if she'd been less timid, or less stupid perhaps (because it's complicated to describe one's feelings), Flo might've allowed herself to speak the way they did. But the conversations going on in that dimly lit waiting room – the kind of conversations for which, perhaps, the yoga had been just a pretext – were too personal, too truthful, as if the desire to talk was not so much the urge to talk as the urge to *relieve themselves*, to *let something out*. After all, wasn't that what yoga was about, wasn't the business of turning oneself upside down and emptying one's head seen to be a form of self-improvement?

Flo sat on the old bench, carved with schoolchildren's graffiti. The yoga instructor sat down beside her. She had a thoughtful expression. What was she thinking about? They were both facing a fish tank in which a dozen or so small yellow fish were, themselves, all facing one direction. Was she wondering what the fish were thinking? What were they thinking? Were they hoping for some miracle to occur? Were they thinking: one day a great tide will come and we will be free? Flo reminded herself of the instructor's name – it's Joy, isn't it? – and thought it an apt name because Joy's body – busty, exuberant, bursting from its clothing – *did* have a joyful quality. Joy's body had an effect on Flo. It made her wish the phone would ring. She wished the phone would ring and was surprised that it didn't, because if the phone was a mental sensation – dependent on her thoughts and feelings – then she ought to have been able, by force of will, to move it the way she could her arm or her leg.

Flo hadn't liked the idea of the phone, exactly, but she preferred the idea of having the phone to not having it. The truth is, she was very *bound up* with the phone. Or rather, the idea of the phone was so *bound up* with her idea of herself that if she didn't have the phone, she wasn't sure she'd have a self any more. So that whereas previously the inner phone had seemed very strange to her, now the memory of its vibrations being transmitted through her blood and nerves was accompanied by a kind of pride, an astonishment, even, at all the incomprehensible things a person can be made up of. She cast her eye into the glowing redness of her inner world. She imagined it nestled somewhere, its screen dark, as if fast asleep. A memory arrived of herself, as a child, being called down a corridor for a long-distance call. Beside her, Joy was putting on a gold helmet. Yes, Joy was gorgeous and you could tell that she liked being gorgeous because she was wearing a complicated gold jumpsuit and putting on that gold helmet. Her body was communicative; it spoke to Flo. When did you stop wanting to be beautiful? it seemed to be asking her. But Flo was reluctant to answer it, because her phone wasn't ringing, if she couldn't speak to whomever had been calling, she didn't want to speak to anybody, because if she couldn't talk about the phone, she wouldn't talk about anything, because she simply didn't know what to say, because what she wanted to say was disgusting (the idea of the phone inside called to the mind all the sordid stories you hear about the things found in women's bodies: car keys, curling tongs . . .) and the phone wasn't disgusting. It was precious. Its secretiveness was what made it so precious.

So pressing were these thoughts that Flo couldn't help saying, almost to herself, I've lost my phone. And Joy, who must have heard her, said Do you want me to call it? And although at first Flo thought, No, then, after a moment, she said, Yes, that would be brilliant. Joy dialled and Flo felt afraid because there had never actually been a phone inside her – of course not, the idea was outrageous! – still, as she waited, her gaze travelled inwards, imagined the phone, its little screen lighting up inside her, and felt a vague panic, a tingling. A phone could not ring unless it has been conceived of in advance. It was her responsibility to have faith in its existence. Of course, it needed someone at the end of the line, but without the preconception, that conversation was just a hope.

SUSTENANCE
Michael Donkor

W HEN people talked about Regina, they said her
name slowly, turning the 'eeeeeee' into a long and
lovely sigh. People said it like that – Reg-eeeeeee-na
– because Regina was beautiful and, perhaps, people felt they
should say her name in a way they thought made it sound
extra special and extra beautiful.

You understood the general view: her face was more
perfect than any other Ghanaian lady's face in south London.
Yes, she could have had her pick. Her dull husband didn't
know his luck.

Sometimes, at church, Regina caught you staring at her
relaxed hair. You couldn't help yourself.

Her relaxed hair.

It glanced off her cheeks and flowed down her magical
neck, her long neck that made her hold her head as if she
were the most super of supermodels.

Because they all loved and were jealous of her, the
aunties had tried hard with their outfits for the christening
of Regina's ugly baby that Sunday. The aunties' headwraps
were higher, their choices of colour cleverer than you'd ever
seen before. Orange stilettos matched with sapphire clutches.
Plum lips, black lips, sin-red lips.

Aunty Gladys – Regina's mother – was swirled up in

lilac and cream, an overgrown tulip at the entrance. She nodded at everyone as they shuffled into St Dunstan's Senior School Hall, specially hired for the party. You watched Aunty Gladys taking compliments and doing catlike things with her hands. When you entered, sticking close to Mum and Dad, Aunty Gladys told you she liked your necklace, but it was very simple: just a little gold cross.

Now, properly in the hall, you loved how it was the same as the playground: the aunties became girls, judging each other with quick looks but pretending they weren't judging each other at all. Your favourites were Aunties Efua and Latrice. They were very old. Maybe forty to fifty years older than Mum, for definite. Or at least their wrinkles made you think that. They were the worst at hiding their watching and judging. It was funny. They were a bit snobby and rude in a good way. They didn't seem to care if anyone knew they were watching and judging. They were fat, old twins, and they lived together because both of their husbands were dead.

At a wedding last year, they were bored and yawning, and you asked why and Aunty Efua said they'd seen it all, seen it all before. But that's impossible, you said, how can you have seen *everything*? And you liked them most at these christenings and funerals and weddings because they some-times let you touch the funny skin on their underarms which was loose and baggy and crêpey, and they always each gave you five pounds which you added to the savings jar beneath your bed.

The uncles were like big kids as well: pretending to be serious in shadowy corners, flapping their robes so they seemed grand and more important than they were, holding Guinness or Supermalt and frowning and nodding and frowning.

You wanted to be involved in it all *so badly*.

You were annoyed Mum had done you up in something so dry – black skirt and white shirt. Mum had said you didn't need to be fancy or attract attention. So you just had to imagine what it would be like to wear long earrings made from peacocks' feathers or to have massively puffed turquoise sleeves.

You were eleven.

Earlier, on the way to the christening and party, on the bus packed with sad, folded-up shoppers, you wanted Mum to tell you what your baptism had been like. Mum only said, 'Small. Quiet.'

Again you asked Mum if, when the new baby came, when your new brother or sister came in three months, if it would have a christening too? You asked her to describe how horrible and hard it was to get a baby out of down there. Like an earthquake – but inside of you?

She only said, 'Hold on to the pole or you will fall and hurt your knees. See us rocking and rolling all around the place. This driver he thinks he is racing Lewis Hamilton.'

Dad had laughed – a little laugh – at the window, at the rain-battered high street outside. He pulled your earlobe. He was in a good mood. He'd polished his shoes nicely – burgundy brogues to match his robes. He'd put in new laces too.

This christening party in the creaky hall was an *OK* party. There were quite a few kids from Sunday School like Damon, and you and Damon were brave and asked the DJing uncle to turn off the Ghanaian music for a few songs and to play Drake instead – and the DJing uncle actually did it! And you drank gallons of Coca-Cola because Coca-Cola was banned at home. So, with Mum busy talking to Aunties Efua and Latrice, the three of them being nearly as serious as the silly, serious men, you and Damon sat with bottles of sugary goodness, imagining the bubbles spiralling into your stomach.

Damon hiccupped a lot and found it hilarious. He kept giggling, gurgling. Each time he hiccupped, he slapped his hands over his mouth like a naughty clown. After he had hiccupped nonstop for about three minutes, you wondered whether it was real or for effect. A lot of the kids from Sunday School thought Damon was stupid. In class, whenever Mrs Carter asked him an easy question Damon's eyes went glassy. Everyone found it annoying because why couldn't he just keep up? Mostly, you thought he was kind and nice. When Mrs Carter told the most horrible Bible stories – what being a slave was actually like, what being crucified was actually like – most people became blank and closed-up. But Damon cried one or two or even three tears. And that was the right thing to do.

But now Damon's burping-hiccupping-whatever was getting really boring. Really boring. Even though it was obvious you weren't enjoying the game, he kept on.

'I need to go to the loo. I'm bursting,' you shouted over the music, getting to your feet.

'Do you want me to come too?' Damon offered.

'No. I'll just be a second. Wait here.'

You could sort of sense his disappointment but didn't care.

✧

You didn't really know the way.

You should have asked one of the tall cousins for help.

The arrows pointed in confusing directions.

The walls were covered with stuff, which wasn't helping either. Year Ten's posters on *A View From The Bridge*. Year Nine's recipes from their charity Great British Bake Off. *Say No To Single-Use Plastic Bottles. Can War Ever Be Just?*

Down more stairs, through some doors, along a corridor and past a growling boiler.

Your bladder was getting properly needy now.

Then more swing doors that opened into a corridor. The only brightness was at the end, the green-white glow of an exit sign. Underneath the sign: a slumped and shifty-shifting thing pressed against the wall. You clicked forward in your Clarks.

Lilac mixed with burgundy.

The one thing split and became two.

First they were holding hands. When they spotted you, they stopped. What light there was caught the smoothness of a man's bald spot and the pointy jewels on a woman's ears.

Lilac mixed with burgundy.

The one thing split and became two.

Dad neatened his robes. Aunty Gladys played with her wrapper skirt. And then they walked towards you. Dad seemed like he was going to hit and hurt. Aunty Gladys was smaller, left him to it. Dad changed, put both hands on your shoulders, smiled at you: a wise man about to give advice.

'Why, why aren't you with your little friends, sweetness? I was . . . helping Aunty Gladys here. She feels very unwell. Unfortunately.'

And Aunty Gladys nodded and did downturned lips. Wilty tulip.

You don't know what came over you. Maybe it was the word 'sweetness' – he had never called you that before. Or maybe it was because of Aunty Gladys's bad acting. Whatever it was, it made you shake off Dad's hands.

You knew how to shake him off but had no clue how to open your mouth. Words appeared in your mind and they travelled through you, deep into your heat, dizziness. They punched their way up your throat and you worried your throat might bleed all over the dark corridor.

In that corridor, with Dad putting his hands back on you and you shaking them off even harder, you thought about earthquakes inside you, volcanoes, Hell. And the words your mind had created stuck to the roof of your mouth and were screaming to get out.

You felt your body's horrible tightness, heat, dizziness. They had made you ill, ill, ill.

What had they given you? Dad. Aunty Gladys. You didn't want what they had given you.

'I. Am. Telling. My. Mum. I'm telling my mum.'

Dad said nothing, only rubbed his bald spot hard and found his genie's lamp wasn't working: no bright ideas. He kissed his teeth. You watched him turn to his nice laces and then he seemed like he was going to hit and hurt again. So you walked down the corridor. You didn't turn back. You didn't know if your body could. At the end of the passage, you pushed the chunky safety bar on the door and stepped into the Teachers' Car Park.

Cold winds, purple sky, dirty clouds. Rectangles marked on the ground in white lines. Orange lights flicked on. They were supposed to make you feel safe but they were frightening. They showed how deep the darkness was.

You wanted to go back inside, get swept up in the Electric Slide, let uncles ask if you were a good girl and drink at least four more cans of Coca-Cola. You wanted sweetness. Your breathing went funny, really, really funny. And in the car park, bumping into elders trying to find their Vauxhall Astras, you waited to cry. It didn't come so you sat down on the ground, right in the middle of a disabled spot. Tarmac was cold against your bum. And wee, warm and ticklish, trickled down your leg. Pooled beneath you. You didn't get up.

✢

The first time you tried to talk to Mum was the next morning. A Monday morning. Mum was getting ready for work.

You followed her.

You waited, hoping she would give you a cue or a nod or a sign to show when she was ready for you to speak.

You kept looking – watching her hands dipping into the moisturiser, watching her guide tights up her legs, watching her trying and failing to pick up Dad's tie, your shorts left on the landing – you kept waiting. Couldn't do it on your own, by yourself.

'You're getting under my feet,' she joked, while she buttoned her big self into her uniform.

'You're like a puppy dog,' she joked, as she did the packed lunches.

'You want to climb into my tummy to join this little one, eh? I don't think I've the space for you too,' she joked, as you trailed behind her, from kitchen to front room, where Lorraine Kelly was getting overexcited about a new kind of Zumba.

When Mum shouted she was leaving, Dad didn't reply.

She kissed your cheek and gave you the permission slip for school. The paper was crushed and warm. You scanned the bit where she had signed her name, near where it always said 'parent/guardian'. You were scared and the hallway seemed narrow, narrow, narrow, as Mum scratched a crumb off one of her front teeth.

You blinked; you gulped.

Mum picked up her keys from the side-table and threw them into her bag. You pulled your shoulders back, put your head up like a soldier. You were brave and right and ready to speak and this was good. You made your hands into fists so your nails pressed into your palms and you stamped on the spot a bit and you didn't know why you did that. You relaxed your fists and you liked the nice loose release and you imagined how that feeling would come to you times ten once you'd done it, once it was done. But then you knew that feeling would last for a second before it was replaced by another. A bigger one. A darker one.

You did not know what to do or what to choose. You wished you didn't know and hadn't seen.

You were scared and the hallway seemed narrow, narrow, narrow, and then Mum checked herself in the mirror.

She was getting really annoyed with her lapel. You noticed her sucking in her cheeks, trying out different smiles. You saw her stretching the skin near her eyes, heard her sigh and slam the door. Your shoulders dropped.

You wanted to hit or hurt yourself.

✧

The next time you properly tried again was at the weekend.

It was Saturday, early evening.

You had spent the afternoon in the local library doing homework, making an A3 poster about Egyptians. You concentrated really hard on the drawings of Nefertiti. When you finished, you got up from the desk and checked what you'd done. You started to hate it and feel weird inside because the page was so crowded with hieroglyphics and cats and bubble writing like you were trying to hide something. And you could hear your heart slapping against the inside of your chest and you nearly ripped the poster but stopped because the librarian with the cheerful freckles said well done and she wished she had handwriting as nice as yours. You sat down among all of the dead shelves with their dead books and dead words.

You wished you had some words. Just a handful. A short sentence might be enough to do the work.

You'd say it once and then you might never have to speak ever again; once, and the effort it took might be so much you would faint, die, disappear, explode.

That would be right.

When you got home, Mum was on the little balcony, hanging up the washing. She called for you to come so you did. You gently pushed her to one side. She sat on the stool Dad put out there for when it was a sunny day and he wanted to read the paper with warmth passing over him. You draped knickers, pants, socks over the clothes line; pinned them in place with Poundland pegs.

When the laundry basket was empty and the line went bendy in the middle, Mum turned to face the estate. The big blocks opposite. The windows winking with light. She put her hand underneath the bump. She held the weight like it was so precious. All she had.

'Can I feel it too, please?'

'Feel? It's not kicking or moving or anything. Nothing to feel.'

'But still. Can I have a go?'

Mum raised an eyebrow. Mum rolled both eyes. Mum nodded. You knelt by her and you carefully patted the huge bulge.

'It's always so hard and . . . eugh! Like an armadillo!'

'Armadillo?' Mum put her hand on top of yours. 'One day it won't seem so strange,' she said. 'You will have your own. You will get used to it. You have to.'

She looked at you like you were the same, on the same level. Or, you would be. Soon.

Her eyes were not in charge or telling off or bossing or homework or chores or prayers before meals or prayers before bed.

Cold winds, purpling sky, dirty clouds.

You slipped your hand away.

'What's the matter?'

'I—'

You blinked, you gulped, you breathed.

You blinked. You gulped. You breathed.

'What on earth is the matter?'

Cold winds, purpling sky, dirty clouds.

Cold winds became faster winds, winds that got crazy and Mum went 'Ey! Ey! Ey!' because a gust stole her T-shirt from the line, sent it wheeling up. Mum grabbed, grabbed, grabbed. The stretch of her arm. The strain in her jaw. The strength of her arm, of her jaw.

'I—'

Mum's big body was so strong, but you were smaller, a tiny child. Know your place.

What place? You looked back at the front room. Not your home any more. Everything had changed. Some other world now.

'Yes, you're right,' Mum collected the basket, nudged you to the door and spoke softly. 'We should go inside. It's cold. Too cold for us out here. Eh?'

÷

Two days later, when you came home from school, you stood in the passageway for a bit, confused. You could hear crying. A baby crying, not a grown-up. The cries were thin and high-pitched. You walked into the living room and Regina and Mum and Dad were there. And Regina's ugly son was throwing his fists around and wriggling.

'Hello and nice to see you,' you muttered, because you were a polite girl. But really, you didn't want to be polite. You wanted to ask Regina if she knew what her mum and your dad had done under the *Exit* sign. You were desperate for Regina to shout. You would take the baby from her and bounce it on your knee while she got up and gave Dad a big piece of her mind. And then once she screamed it all out and flashed her eyes to curse his soul and tossed her relaxed hair, you would pass the baby back, mouth 'thank you' and show her out.

'Hello and nice to see you also. I'm just paying visits to the christening guests. Saying thank you.' Regina's voice was so pretty, prettier even than her shiny, peach nails that reminded you of pearls. So delicious. Every time the baby cried, everyone did excited noises like they were impressed by how much noise he could make. Everyone smiled but Regina's smile was the biggest and falsest one. The baby screamed more, seemed to hate his mother's grin.

'Oh, don't worry, Reg-eeeeeee-na. It gets easier,' Mum promised. Her voice didn't believe itself.

You asked if they wanted more tea.

'I will help you prepare it,' Dad offered.

In the kitchen – getting the good spoons, good mugs – he was as silent as he had been every other day since you spotted him doing his nastiness. He bumped into you when reaching for the chocolate biscuits but didn't say excuse me or anything.

He poured the hot water into the cups.

He gave you the damp little teabags to throw away.

Like everything was normal.

As you poured in the milk, he told you to be careful in case you ruined it for everyone. His voice was too heavy when he spoke. Your hands shook.

When you went back into the front room – Dad holding the door open for you – neither Regina nor the baby were there. Mum saw your surprise.

'She is changing him in the bathroom. He did a little poo-poo.'

Dad laughed at the silliness of the word. And all the time, you heard the baby's anger upstairs, a noise spilling and spilling and pressing on your mind.

You did your best to rest the tray on the coffee table carefully, then sat on the little pouffe to unbuckle your Mary Janes. And Mum and Dad were still laughing at the word poo-poo and the bigness of the baby's lungs. In your mind, a mind squashed by a baby's screams, you couldn't get rid of a picture: Regina's nails having to deal with all of the brown muck. And everyone just laughing and telling her it'll get easier.

You turned to Dad. You stared. Pointed with a wobbly finger.

'Are you, are you feeling quite well, my child?' His eyes were doing a lot – going between scared and bossy and testing.

'I'm. Fine. *You.*'

And when he tried to come over, like he was going to check the warmth of your forehead to see if you were ill, you got up and shuffled back from him and banged your head against the cabinet. Your pointing finger crumpled.

'You don't—' Mum whispered.

With your dad reaching towards you and your own hand trying to soften the soreness, you saw a frowning Mum and stupid Dad. Useless. You sank and thudded into the pouffe. Mum said you were too young to be doing teenage nonsense.

The crying stopped. Now Regina and the baby came back. Regina had a different smile and returned to the sofa; the baby in her arms flopped obediently. The adults went back to talking about nothing, pushing more sugary biscuits between their lips. The baby's little arm lolled around – a king waving to crowds – and spit dribbled from the corner of his white-crusty mouth. Dad gently tucked the baby more neatly into the bright cloths he was wrapped in. Called him a 'good boy, really'.

✛

Three days later, it was the middle of the night and you woke up because it got *cooler*.

Suddenly it wasn't nice and warm and toasty but cooler. Icy toes and ankles. The duvet had been peeled back. You tugged the sheets and tried to re-cover yourself but couldn't because of something holding the bedclothes tight.

You didn't like it one bit.

'Shh. OK. OK?'

'Oh!'

Mum's whispering voice was crisp and sharp and pointy. Mum clicked on your lamp. She had your coat over one arm. She made a motion with her other hand. Her eyes said things that were crisp and sharp and pointy. She put her fingers to her lips like it was Assembly. You put your fingers on your lips too.

She pointed to your Nikes and you put them on.

She gave you your coat and you buttoned it up.

She carefully opened your wardrobe and in the bottom there was a big rucksack you had never seen before, big and black and really full. Mum pointed at it and you laced your arms through the straps. It was as heavy as you thought it was going to be. You worried you were going to make a moany noise because of the weight, but you didn't.

Mum tiptoed. Her big body did its best to be as small as it could as they walked past Mum and Dad's room and then the bathroom. And you followed her and mirrored her, your whole body tense too, as she grabbed, grabbed, grabbed, more rucksacks hidden in the little airing cupboard.

And you crept down the stairs, still holding your muscles tight and working your hardest so nothing rustled or creaked. You held your breath. You watched where your feet went. Tight shadows shifted around you. At the bottom of the stairs, Aunties Efua and Latrice waited and did a beckoning thing with their hands, inviting you both down, asking you to come, and fast.

Whipping the air with their hands. Whipping it, whipping it, whipping it.

'UNCLE' BILL
Benjamin Markovits

I ALWAYS called him Bill Anderson because my parents in his absence at the dinner table referred to him always by his full name. So that's what I called him to his face, hi Bill Anderson, and at a certain point he said Bill is fine. He was maybe their best friend in a city (Austin) where they moved because they both got jobs and could afford a nice house and where a social life was not the priority. My parents had a lot of kids. They had real affection for the place, which did not rule out long-term frustrations and disappointments with the life available to them there.

Bill Anderson always seemed less frustrated and disappointed. When we were kids he had a hip, cute girlfriend named Rachel, a red-head, who joked in my presence (I was sitting in the backseat of a car) about a friend of hers who broke up with a guy because of . . . and the private look they shared (in the front seat) represented in my mind for many years the secret world of adulthood, with all its mysterious illicit forces. It wasn't really private, it was just the look you give around kids when you say something not in the voice you say to them but to another grown-up in the room.

But they broke up, and Bill Anderson became what my mother liked to call an eligible bachelor – to express affection for him and also a certain limit to her interest in that side of his life. He had a good job at the law school, he read the *New York Times* and the *New Yorker* and the National Book Award winners, and bought expensive photographs from up-and-coming photographers. Also, if there was an exercise fad going, he was ready to try it. Boxercise, jazzercise. The relationship with Rachel didn't last for reasons I had no clue about and couldn't have understood if my parents had explained it to me at the time, which I'm sure they didn't. Maybe he didn't want to have kids, and she did. Anyway, he never had kids.

He used to come round to our house on certain family occasions, Thanksgiving sometimes, after Christmas, but most often to watch a ball game. Sometimes at half time we wandered outside into the mild Texas evening air to shoot hoops with my dad, and Bill played with a herky-jerky old-school style that made him look like his joints needed oiling. In his day, he insisted, everybody played like that. His dance card was always full; we were just one of the dances. Bill was also involved in several book groups, whose members included Nobel Prize-winners from other departments at the university. When he came for dinner, he often brought along something he wanted to show me, something he thought I should read, because I liked poetry, and my tastes were old-fashioned. Mostly because of the limiting influence of my parents. For example, he gave me the complete works of Walt Whitman one day and read out at the dinner table in a strong natural American accent, 1942 vintage:

> The young men float on their backs, their white bellies
>   bulge to the sun, they do not ask who seizes fast to
>   them,
> They do not know who puffs and declines with the pendant
>   and bending arch,
> They do not think whom they souse with spray.

Politely, I always resisted these attempts to shape my literary interests, but afterwards when he was gone, and sometimes several years later, came back to the poems he had shown me, remembered them, thought about why he had liked them, and changed my mind. He had very good taste. Sometimes I bugged my parents to join in his reading groups, as a way to get them out of the house, but I didn't think they'd really like it, and I didn't bug hard. I wouldn't have gone to them either.

As a family we always responded to Bill's cultural enthusiasms with slight but fond embarrassment. Have you read *American Psycho*? he asked us over dessert. If we had we'd argue with him about it or even if we hadn't. But I don't think it bothered him. He was either deaf to our tone of superior indifference or felt superior to it himself, which is what he should have felt.

✢

When I came back from college, he had a wife, who was ten years older than him and much admired by my parents. They took a collective view of her as a substantial person. Bill hired a prominent local architect to improve and expand his living-room area, enclosing a courtyard, which could be viewed on three sides through glass panels, and opening out and modernising the central fireplace. It seemed magically suspended two feet above the ground. They bought a Winogrand. I rarely visited him at home, maybe once or twice for brunch on New Year's Day, where he showed me new additions to his collection. He liked to support local artists and I didn't know their names. There were photographs and paintings – and sculptures in the stone-filled courtyard, which was also filled with clear winter sunlight and large succulent plants. His wife baked and cooked and everything she made was excellent.

When she died of cancer a few years later it forced my

parents to expose to their friend their unreserved affection for him and unhesitating warm feeling, which for the greater part of their relationship they had partly covered up. Like people who wear their coat or jacket even inside, because they still feel a little cold or don't want to bother to make their host hang it up, or because they still feel like they're in some kind of public space and wearing the jacket or coat is a way of making other people feel it too. Bill spoke of his dead wife with complete admiration; she not only shared but continually informed and enriched his taste and view of the world. They had a lot of fun, too. They travelled a lot. They went to New York and took in a lot of shows. They tracked down exhibitions they wanted to see in places like The Hague. And afterwards, always, they came to the house I grew up in and wanted to talk about them and hear what we thought.

After her death, he still came over, usually to watch a ball game. He still brought me books to read, if he knew I was in town. He introduced me to 'Gravy' by Raymond Carver, about a guy who sobers up after the doctors give him six months, and lives eleven more years. Gravy means something extra, it's what you get on top of everything else, another decade of conscious, loving, high-quality existence. But Bill meant *her*, his wife, whose medical sentence had been issued in this way, and whose late arrival on the scene of his life granted him those years. At half time, we still walked outside in the evening air to shoot hoops, across the sharp-leaved Texas lawn, under the pecan tree, even though he could barely make it to the court now. His breathing was like the description in 'Kubla Khan', intermitted, loud and thick, after a rare genetic condition or viral infection had gripped him in the lungs, in all the convoluted branch and root system of alveoli and capillaries, until the doctors cut him open and took out half. Let me make a shot before going in, he said, and stiff-armed the ball into the rim. Give me another, breathing heavy, jerking his shoulders back, shooting again and again until the ball rolled in. I can't watch college hoops any more, he said. They're just kids, they don't know what they're doing.

Later, years later, he had a triple-bypass operation at a hospital in Dallas that specialised in or pioneered the treatment. His American health insurance was very good, the benefits of teaching at a law school. But the pressure on his lungs, the continual failure of his oxygen supply – do you know what a moiety is? he said to me, taking pleasure in the word, a thing that can be divided into two parts, where the moiety is one of the parts, *a moiety* – had put a strain on his heart that no medicine could cure. *A part or portion* was the dictionary definition, *especially a lesser share.*

He called my father from the hospital bed. 'I've joined the zipper club,' he said.

÷

When I came home at Christmas, he had another girlfriend. The beautiful Claire, my father had decided to call her, the way I used to call him Bill Anderson – as if that were his working title. An elegant southerner, in her seventies, she had been a diplomat's wife and lived in Washington and Hong Kong. In Paris, also, she had memories and associations and places she liked to go, and she knew interesting and significant people, like the Pinskys. They lived separately but came to dinner together and wanted to talk art and books and movies and politics. I said to him, how are you doing, how do you feel, and he quoted at me a line he'd read in the *New Yorker* that week or heard at a concert in Portland, some kind of experimental electropop, I can't remember – *Feeling good about feeling good*. At a certain age, he said, that's enough, that's all you can hope for.

A few years ago he came to tea at my house in London. Like I was a grown-up finally and not the kid who could disappear into his room. They didn't stay to dinner because they had to catch a flight to Istanbul early the next morning. He wanted to see the Topkapi Palace, walk through the *cicek pasaji* (the flower passage, he said, translating) and visit the Museum of Innocence. 'Have you read the novel?' They arrived at Atatürk Airport on 27 June, a day before the terrorist attack, and afterwards spent two weeks in the country, travelling. He sent me an email with a photo of the pair of them, in front of a palace or temple. 'The buildings are turtles,' was all he wrote. Not bad for a kid from Maple Shade, New Jersey, was how I read the subtext, though maybe this is more the kind of thing my father would have said.

✢

The last time I saw Bill was in Manhattan. He and Claire wanted to take in a little jazz, and came to dinner at my sister-in-law's apartment (it's a long story, with multiple connecting threads). We ate Cuban Chinese. They stayed for an hour; he tired easily and wanted to save his energy for the Village. His interest in these things was indefatigable.

After a lung transplant, they put him on immunosuppressants to keep his body from rejecting the organ. One of the side effects was that he had to be very careful around people with colds, and also in sunshine. His pale skin sprouted melanomas like moss in wet grass, which the doctors periodically removed. One of them metastasised. My parents usually spend the summer in London, and for several weeks my father called him daily in his hospital room. Sometimes he was with it, sometimes he wasn't. I don't know how intimate their conversations were. My father was checking up, dutifully, and I was often surprised by the limits he considered natural in his conversations with male friends. What happened next happened in a kind of rapid slow motion. Somehow you were complicit, because you could see it happening and there was nothing you could do. One day Bill was dead.

A few weeks later my parents returned to Austin and the city was emptier than it had been, my father said. The place where by chance they had made their lives was missing one of the people chance had thrown them in with. When you're a kid, in school, everybody you know is in your class, and out of these materials you build a childhood, and the kids you know stand for all the human varieties, and that seems like enough; you never have such friendships again, because of the forced shared life, seven hours a day, watching the same teachers, doing the same things, practising your personality on these events. But then in adulthood the same thing happens. You move somewhere for practical reasons, because of a job, and instead of seven hours a day in the same place what you have is fifty years.

One of the first books Bill bought me (I was thirteen years old) still sits on my desk when I write. An anthology of American verse – the cover is a painting by Robert Rauschenberg. Bill came into the house, ringing the bell and opening the front door at the same time, walking through the hall towards the TV room, thumbing the book open at the page he wanted to show me. His lungs worked, his heart beat, his skin was clear – he was something like my age now. He wore a moustache then and read out to me, through the soft hairs, as I turned down the sound of the ball game:

> Captain Carpenter rose up in his prime,
> Put on his pistols and went riding out . . .

By John Crowe Ransom, where the valiant captain, chasing the Grail and continually defeated, forfeits at every turn a piece of his body, but rides on with whatever he has left until the bastards take his heart.

After his death, a local museum inherited his collection, and the executor went around Bill's house to take stock. My parents were invited, too, and saw a picture my sister once painted of him, years ago, when she minored in painting at university and needed subjects. Can we have that? they asked. Really, it was supposed to go to the museum, but the executor said (a little snobbishly, they told me), 'I don't think anyone will miss it.' So they took it home and gave it back to her. My sister edits an Austin literary magazine; Bill left them some money, too. At first she didn't remember painting it and then suddenly she did. It hangs over her desk now; she looks at it every day and reminded me somewhat ruefully, by email when I sent her this piece, of a Larkin line that Bill liked to misquote: *What will survive of us is art.*

THE MINING DISASTER

Alex Preston

WHEN the earth began to wrench and roil, we grabbed at solid things: stalagmites, wooden pillars, the heavy trucks that began to buck and rear on the tracks. Some of us lay on the ground, huddled in tight curls as dust and rock showered from the roof. It was as if our ship had been whelmed in a rolling ocean, and everything we reached for betrayed us, revealing itself as shifting and insubstantial. A breathless explosion, a rush of noxious air. Silence. We sniffed, our lips puckering. Firedamp reaching its foul fingers through the darkness towards us. Then a more precipitous shift of the earth and, with a groan and a roar, the coalface began to crumble, the tunnel floor disappearing with it. The trucks clashed and chimed as they toppled, throwing up sparks that threatened to ignite the gassy air. Falling men were visible in the yawning void only by the beams of their headlamps, like hopeless ropes thrown to shore. So many, so many tossed in the dark flood. In that second silence, we looked around. Eighteen lamps, perched on the lip of the abyss. Before, there'd been fifty of us. Below, now, we could hear running water, the lazy settling of the rocks, a single man calling out. *Mama, oh help me, Mama.* We clung to one another like children.

✣

You don't remember your parents' faces. They are rounded up in the great Vel d'Hiv *rafle* of '42. The concierge hides you in the nook of a fireplace, a wardrobe hefted in front of it. You sometimes wonder why you can still remember the grain of the wardrobe's wood on your fingertips, the whirls and whorls that you trace in the darkness, and yet, when you look at the photograph of your parents that Madame Delphy gives you, slightly blurred, your mother in white organdie, your father in shirtsleeves, you can find no bridge that will allow them into your memory.

For the rest of the war the concierge keeps you concealed in her apartment. Madame Delphy has an ear for trouble and, whenever rumours circulate of a *rafle* or a *razzia* (the latter phrase adopted by Parisian police from the Foreign Legion's colonial adventures), she ushers you into the dark burrow behind the wardrobe. For days you crouch there, afraid to stretch or sniffle, cups of water and crumbling *tartines* passed to you by the kindly, quiet concierge. Sometimes, when the light behind her seems blindingly bright after hours in the blackness, you think she's your mother come back to save you.

Madame Delphy is a collector, her rooms on the ground floor act as a glory-hole into which flow the abandoned goods of the higher apartments. When someone dies, or, like your parents, disappears, the choicest pieces find themselves squirrelled down to rest in the care of the concierge. There, in the dim and dusty half-light, you ride on a child's tricycle – too small for you – squeaking between collections of quartzes and precious stones, Meissen figurines and antique dolls. Stopping to inspect the military paraphernalia, you fix a plumed shako bobbing on your head; then you wheel into the room of clocks, whose syncopated tickings accompany your first dance steps. You spend hours with the astrolabe, the barometer with hydrographic chart, the maps of the Ptolemeic constellations.

Most often, though, you sit at your father's roll-top desk, looking into the light well, waiting for the few minutes each day, fewer in winter, when the sun floods the building's shaft with brightness, and all the glittering things in Madame Delphy's collection come alive. Mirrors pass beams of light between them, the quartzes quiver and gleam, the nacreous inlays of pocket watches, jewellery boxes, cigarette cases, commence a glowing dance.

Now when you're asked by a journalist, or during the introductory forays of a conference, before you begin to expostulate on horsts and grabens, magmatism and alkali basalts, what was it that brought you to geology, you speak of those few minutes of brightness, of the sun arrowing down into the light well, the shaft filling with light. The regularity of those moments, the expectation and fulfilment, they have given a shape to your mind, a shading – height and depth, light and darkness – which you now find in the rifts and runnels of the earth.

✣

We edged along the narrow ridge – all that was left of the tunnel – imagining ourselves on a mountainside above a roaring cataract, each urging the next not to look down into the blackness where, still, the dying voice of a man, his head-lamp swinging from side to side in his agony. We reached the foot of the shaft where the tunnel opened out, allowing us to stand straight, to take stock of the devastation. Timbering and brattice all piled in sulking heaps. Shining our lights upward, we could see that the walls of the shaft had pressed together like two hands in prayer. One of us began to cry, and that was all right, because it drowned out the distant screams of the dying man, the rush of the water which had grown to a galloping torrent in the chasm below. Still the foetid fog in the air, the dust raining from the roof, which caught in our beards, silted up our noses and mouths, crusted in the corners of our eyes. We stood there, looking hopelessly upwards, as if suddenly aware of how lost, how alone, how abandoned we were. Down there in the darkness, we could feel the movement of the hurtling earth, the lonely spin of our dying planet. In the silent blackness of the mine we could imagine how it will be when everything is ended, when the sun expires, and where once there were stars there is only an aching and eternal void.

❖

You start school in the spring of 1946, Mme Delphy packing you off with your sandwiches wrapped in greaseproof paper, a cap skew-whiff on your fuzzy brush of hair. In the evenings, she greets you with a kiss and a *goûter* of hot chocolate and *langues de chat*. You sit at the kitchen table in close, happy silence. In 1949, she dies of a subarachnoid haemorrhage, and you win a bursary to the Collège Stanislas. Five lonely years in the scholars' dormitory overlooking the Rue Notre-Dame-des-Champs. The wind picks up speed over the Luxembourg Gardens, meets little resistance in the draughty shuttered windows of the dormitory, and gusts across the beds of the twelve boys. You shiver yourself to sleep. Then it is Jussieu, Paris-Diderot, further research at the Sorbonne. You specialise in optical mineralogy and crystal structure, write a well-received paper on isomorphism in clay. You leave the Sorbonne before finishing your doctorate and take up a position at the Société Peñarroya, swiftly rising to become Chief Mineralogist.

I can see you now, in a suit of grey worsted, your hair's unruly squiggles tamped by a felt fedora. On your face, a certain melancholy distance which means that your colleagues don't ask you to join them for coffee at eleven, wine at five. You return through dusky streets to the apartment you now lease on the third floor of the same block in which you grew up. You put music on the gramophone, lay your crystals on your father's roll-top desk (recovered from an antique dealer on the Avenue Kléber), and turn them under the light of a green-shaded lawyer's lamp: uvarovite druzes, dolomite geodes, pink pyrite vugs in which you place now one finger, now two, running your nails over the reticulated inner surfaces. You sit until the small hours of the morning, looking out into the shadowy light well, and the music plays on.

✢

We knelt and prayed, extending our arms towards the crumbling roof, and soon we were covered in fine dust, like plaster icons. One of the men, Karel, wondered aloud if they would be heard, our prayers, from such a distance, through the strata of compacted rock. We ignored him and raised our voices above the roar of the water. Later, we crawled to the edge of the ravine and stared downwards, stretched out on our stomachs like young tykes spying on sunbathing girls. The black water reflected our torches, we saw occasional islands of coal and rock, soon swallowed by the rising flood. We were all struck by the abysmal horror of it – the depths, the darkness, the water. The river gushed up from the rocks to the western end of the ravine; we could dimly make out the point, off to the east, where it disappeared again under the earth, entering the mouth of a tunnel. The water had swept away the screaming man. There was no sound from above, no drilling or distant voices, only the sense of a whole forgetful world pressing down upon us. *We are lost*, Karel cried out, and no one would comfort him. I, the oldest among us, lifted my hands and began to pray again, sucking the afterdamp into my lungs and pouring out *De profundis clamavi ad te, Domine: Domine, exaudi vocem meam.*

✢

It is in 1976, during a visit to one of the Societé's open-cast copper mines in Wallis and Futuna, that you feel the first jostlings of the obsession that will come to shape your life. Six miners have been trapped in a cut-and-cover trench, the wood of the support beams worm-rotted and friable. There, cupped in the palm of the mine, in the boiling heat, with the screams of the trapped men in your ears, you are hit with a vision that seems to come into your mind fully formed and thoughtless. You perceive how the surrounding geological stress of the rock might be used to support the tunnel, to free the men. You set a team working with rock bolts and mesh. You feel buoyed up, invincible. As the last stones are lifted away, you step like a god into the mouth of the cave and lead the men out, blinking, newborn into the brightness.

If this were a film, I would show you first back in Paris, at a workbench, your pen a grey blur as you sketch cross-sections and geomechanical diagrammes, early setbacks prompting greater leaps forward. Now, on a turning globe, Air France jetliners ferry you to disasters in Abidjan and Yaoundé, in Linares and Santa Cruz de la Sierra, to Dumas and Plainview. You are there, in khaki, a cowboy hat on the frizzy hair that is now zagged through with silver. The stones are rolled away – employing your patented method – and you step in, smiling, and lead the survivors out. You like to sit with them afterwards as they weep and hug their wives, press their damp cheeks to those of their bright-eyed children, lie with their heads in their mothers' laps. You remember a vision you had of your own mother, come to rescue you from behind the wardrobe as a child, and you want to be here for these moments, when all that was feared lost is recovered, and you can cry with them, press yourself into the soft heat of their love.

✢

Some scenes from Tartarus: three days had passed. We'd finished our drinking water, the hardtack that one of us had kept in a pocket. Then the thirst came, and we looked down into the rising waters of that underground river and almost willed them upwards, even while knowing what would happen when the water crested the lips of the ravine. We all, at the same moment, imagined pressing our mouths into the last few inches of air at the top of the cave, the murky sight of each other underwater, our limbs drifting like weeds in the ghostly green. One of the men went mad. He ran at the mound of rocks and debris at the foot of the shaft, scrabbling at it with his hands, mewling like a cat. We had to tie him up. I drew my knife and cut lengths of rope, bound his feet and hands fast. His name was Branislav. A big, burly boy. When he continued to scream, rolling on the ground like an imbecile, I, as the eldest, took charge. Grabbing him by his bound feet, I dragged him to the edge of the rock face and pitched him off. His screaming didn't change one bit, not until he was under the water and gone. I turned to look at the other men. One of them shrugged. *Pray*, I said. *Branislav didn't pray hard enough.* All seventeen of us, on our knees again, offering up our alleluias and Hail Marys and Anima Christis. I felt, inside me then, a knot of certainty growing. That this was what my life had been leading towards, that this flooding mine was to be the scene of my glory.

✣

You are flown into Čáslav Airport in a Breguet 941. Your assistant, Bruno, has radioed ahead with instructions to the site team. You are forty-six, single, wealthy. In the years since you began working at the firm, Société Peñarroya has been taken over by Damrec and then reverse-merged into the Imerys conglomerate, but your arm of the business – Mine Safety Solutions, S.A. – has continued its uninterrupted ascent. Now, as Germany slips by beneath, you sift through reams of file notes and technical data until you understand the situation in the collapsed mine down to the most minute detail, and this pleases you. You picture yourself as a surgeon operating on the heart of the earth: instead of scalpels, you have auger bits, instead of stents you have pipe-jacking. You are about to extend the metaphor further in your mind when the plane hits an eddy of turbulence, a delicious lurch where you feel the sudden precariousness of being airborne. Then the plane wheels down, down, like a gull, like a tern, and with three sharp bumps and a squeal of rubber on tarmac, you have arrived.

A car is waiting to hurry you along the *dálnice*. A ribboned functionary of the CSSR sits beside you, asks you, in English, to sign documents ensuring *complete* – he jabs the word with his finger – confidentiality. You have worked with the Russians, you tell him. You know the drill. You smile; he doesn't. You lean back and look out of the window: a brief glimpse of the Elbe, then endless forests of melancholy white birches, drab towns rising like dreams from the flat landscape. A thick mantle of fog lies over the land around the Sokolov Mine. You pass between two watchtowers poking up out of the murk. Intimations of the blasted landscape around. Then, as the car – a well-upholstered Dacia – slows, you make out through the fog the usual gaggle of press and politicians, the miners' families who stand in silent, watchful clusters. As you step out into the damp air, they look at you with fretful, fearful hope.

✢

We lost another three men to the river. Two of them, brothers, Serbs I think (they muttered and grunted to each other, barely spoke to us), chanced themselves to the water. They stood on the cusp of the ravine like angels on the rim of a cloud, clasped each other by the hand and jumped. We shone our torches down upon them, but their grip must have slipped, because only one brother was visible, grabbing onto a slab of rock and drinking greedily, his face in the river like a pig in its trough. Then a surge of water and he let go, looking up at us, and we saw him disappear into the mouth of the tunnel. I imagined the two boys, like tongues in the river's throat, sliding onwards, onwards, praying for a break in the rock, then the release of breath, the white choke of the water, and still, even though life had left them, sliding on, deeper, in utter darkness. The third man – Karel – wouldn't pray with us. Now there were thirteen men left, and me. I held my knife in one hand. In the other I waved a cigarette lighter, tracing patterns in the afterdamp as we prayed: green and crimson and sulphurous yellow flames that shifted and glowed. As I wrapped the colours around me, I pictured myself as a bird of some deep paradise, decked in plumage of iridescent light. The men looked to me as their father, reaching up to touch my beard as, one by one, I judged them, and found them wanting.

✣

The collapse of the shaft proves more difficult than you'd imagined, the rock more porous and granular, the angles of incidence more acute. You install double telescopic jacks, relay bars, a reverse-mounted ram that begins to pump away at the knitted earth, throwing up great joyful clouds of rock and soil. You make a tour of the families, examining the wives in their damp eyes, letting your gloved hand rest on the heads of the children. After three hours, a breach is made in the rock and you oversee the insertion of steel castings. The shaft becomes wider, wide enough for the lift mechanism. You remove the yellow safety helmet and wipe a sleeve across your brow.

✣

You insisted on being the first to descend; this was your indulgence, your katabasis: a trip to the land of the dead. The lift machinery clanked and thunked as you passed out of sight of those above ground. Rocks crumbled and shifted, but you were sure of the shaft's integrity, certain of your own calculations. You practised the face you would show to us, the saved – benevolent and wise. There were bottles of water at your feet, flashlights, medical packs. The lift reached the dusty floor of the cave with a rumble. A moment's pause. You could hear the rushing of the water, could see the river that was already slopping over the edge of the cliff-face; then you turned towards me.

÷

It takes your habitual face a careful moment before it adjusts to the scene. I stand there, have been standing waiting ever since the first distant thuds came to us, five hours earlier. I have been writing your story. The air around me is plumed through with colour, great swirls of light that illuminate my eyes, my beard. A shimmering green cloud seems to hover above me, brooding over the scene. I am alone, the prophet of these dark reaches. All the others, all my scared and sinful children, are deep in the belly of the earth.

I don't know if the tale I have invented for you is the right one, or if maybe the man now standing on the lift platform before me is instead a Silesian mine-owner, a German medic, an English aid-worker. But I am pleased with the shape and scope of the story I have given you, and so, when you try to speak, to cry out and reveal your language, I spring forward and press my palm across your mouth, my knife to your throat. Yours is the last body I heave into the water. I watch you go, my child, your body bobbing for a while before the current really takes it, and you are sucked down into the earth's black maw.

I send the lift back up, empty. Then I stand in the heart of the technicolour clouds, running the point of my knife across my palm, and I begin another story, my mind spooling out and up into the world of endless possibilities, the world above ground.

✢

You are born in the military hospital in Prague – your father is an officer, your mother a ballerina at the conservatory, only just seventeen. Within hours of your birth, you are spirited through the snowy night to the Carmelites at the Cloister of the Infant Jesus of Prague. They name you Marek, no, Kazimir, no, Roman. Even as a child, you are drawn to wounded, fragile things. Now you step onto the platform that has appeared in the mouth of the shaft. You stand on the small metal lift and you begin to descend – clunk, clunk, clunk – and as I wait for you, my beard dripping, the waters slopping, my palms held out, I tell your story.

REALMS OF GOLD

Sarah Churchwell

1924

—

I N December 1924, Scott Fitzgerald and his wife Zelda
were living in the Hotel des Princes, a small, unfashionable but comfortable – and affordable – hotel in Rome,
on the west side of the Spanish Steps. Across the steps, on
the east, stood the Casina Rossa, the house in which John
Keats had died a century before. The Fitzgeralds had chosen
the Piazza di Spagna for its proximity to the ghost of Keats.
This was no mere touristic gesture: Fitzgerald's feeling for
Keats went beyond appreciation, or even love, into a kind of
literary fealty. Keats, it has been said, was the greatest poet
of pleasure in our tradition. Pleasure was not something he
merely felt, but something he understood: exaltation as a
moral response to the joy of existence, a natural state of
intoxication.

The Fitzgeralds had come to Rome from the French
Riviera in November after Fitzgerald submitted the manu-
script of his third novel, so he could complete revisions for
publication in the spring. This novel used Keats throughout,
threading allusions and updatings, turning romantic poetry
into roaring jazz. As of the beginning of December, Fitzgerald
was still vacillating over his novel's title, writing to his editor
that maybe it should simply be called *Trimalchio* – or perhaps
just *Gatsby*. He couldn't decide. But one thing he believed:

'I think my novel is about the best American novel ever written,' he confessed to his editor.

Two weeks later, Fitzgerald wrote another letter from the Hotel des Princes, this one a simple note of thanks to a translator who had sent him a new edition of a volume of Sappho's poems. 'The Sappho followed me around Europe and reached me here,' he said. 'It's gorgeous – I'd always wanted to read Sappho but I never realised it would be such a pleasure as you've made it.' He closed by thanking the translator, John Myers O'Hara, for his courtesy in sending the copy.

Some years later, it seems, Fitzgerald sent O'Hara a reciprocal volume: in this case, an inscribed copy of his own first novel, *This Side of Paradise*. ('It was always the becoming he dreamed of, never the being,' he writes of its protagonist.) What prompted the gift is unclear, but Fitzgerald inscribed it in 'Washington D.C.', which means it was likely sent sometime between 1930 and 1935, by which point the Fitzgeralds were living in Baltimore.

The inscription read: 'For John Myers O'Hara, who first introduced me to Sappho in his translations, with a thousand thanks. "Much have I travelled in the realms of gold . . ." His most cordially, F. Scott Fitzgerald, Washington D.C.'

You'd think that a translator of ancient Greek would have appreciated the compliment, but you'd be wrong. In 1935, the book was auctioned. It wouldn't have got much.

But it begins a story riddled with quotations, quotations that form riddles. Riddle, derived from the Old German for *read*.

1816
—

I N the autumn of 1816, John Keats spent the evening with a school friend who had been lent a sumptuously illustrated folio book published 200 years earlier. Its title page, styled 'The Whole Works of Homer: Prince of Poetts In his Iliads, and Odysses, Translated according to the Greek by Geo. Chapman', was embellished with drawings of heroes and gods, along with several Latin mottos, working as early blurbs. The largest one, *'qui nil molitur inepte'*, is how Horace described Homer: 'one whose efforts are always successful'.

Keats was acutely aware of the question of literary success. His impecunious family had pushed him to become a doctor, in the hope that it would help them achieve financial security, but he desperately wanted to write poetry. All that autumn night, aspirant, glimmering, he sat poring over the 1616 folio with his friend Charles Cowden Clarke, 'shouting with delight as some passage of especial energy struck his imagination', Clarke later remembered. Here, at last, was what he had been seeking, a catalyst to spark his own genius into life. Here, at last, he found inspiration.

For someone who had only encountered Homer through the pale Augustan precision of Alexander Pope, Chapman's Homer was nothing less than an epiphany. Keats was left 'exclaiming', Clarke recalled, startled into 'one of his delighted stares', by lines such as this description of shipwrecked Odysseus: 'the sea had soak'd his heart through'. They had Pope's translation open nearby for comparison; it rendered the same phrase 'his swoln heart heav'd'.

To be fair to Pope, the words swollen and heaved certainly suggest waves and tempests as well as heavy hearts. But how much more propulsive and memorable is that figurative, alliterative doubling of the sea soaking everything, including the hero's heart. Here was poetry with its pulses pounding, its fingers trembling.

At 'day-spring', after a night spent reading aloud, his heart soaked with words, his mind filled with 'teeming wonderment', Keats strode home, a poem forming in his mind. The draft survives, and shows that he wrote it almost without correction, the poem pouring from him like the imaginary waves that had inspired it.

'On First Looking Into Chapman's Homer' is widely considered Keats's first great poem, the initial step from promise into genius. And what makes it so marvellous (literally, *to be marvelled at*) is that it is a poem about marvel, and revelation. It's about suddenly discovering – not what you've been looking for but rather, what so surpasses your meagre imagination that it leaves you breathless, staring, silent.

Except it left John Keats anything but silent. A few hours later, Clarke said, he came downstairs to find a sonnet awaiting him with his breakfast.

> Much have I travell'd in the realms of gold,
> And many goodly states and kingdoms seen;
> Round many western islands have I been
> Which bards in fealty to Apollo hold.
> Oft of one wide expanse had I been told
> That deep-brow'd Homer ruled as his demesne;
> Yet did I never breathe its pure serene
> Till I heard Chapman speak out loud and bold:
> Then felt I like some watcher of the skies
> When a new planet swims into his ken;
> Or like stout Cortez when with eagle eyes
> He star'd at the Pacific – and all his men
> Look'd at each other with a wild surmise –
> Silent, upon a peak in Darien.

Here is the sudden exhilaration of sensing worlds to conquer; but here also is not understanding until you understand; there's a reason 'comprehend' means both *understand* and *encompass*. Indeed, the line 'never did I breathe its pure serene' originally read: 'Yet could I never tell what men might mean'. Often Keats had heard of Homer's greatness, but never had he felt it, never had he breathed its essence, until Chapman spoke out 'loud and bold' into the stillness.

Speaking in the first person, Keats merges the voice of the poet with that of the voyager into new lands, the discoverer of 'realms of gold', the golden dawn of a new age of poetry. His wonder at encountering new lands, new oceans, was his wonder at discovering new possibilities for poetry. This poem announced not merely Keats's arrival as a poet, but his ability to ascend artistic peaks.

It is about odysseys of discovery, of a world suddenly enlarged, expanded. This is why it's so apt that Keats's master metaphor comes from Homer, and that he keeps his metaphors so strictly within the realms of exploration. Here was no mere attempt, no feeble velleity. Here was the grandeur of endeavour – like the famous voyage of the *Endeavour*, in which Captain Cook set sail to a different new world in 1768. 'On First Reading Chapman's Homer' left its first readers similarly struck dumb, standing before an enormous vista of poetic possibility.

Two years later, Keats's brother George voyaged to the United States. Whatever his faith in the inspirational power of imaginary Americas, Keats was considerably less sanguine about the real thing. Although some believed 'that America will be the country to take up the human intellect where England leaves off', he begged to differ:

A country like the United States whose greatest Men are Franklins and Washingtons will never do that. They are great Men doubtless but how are they to be compared to those our countrymen Milton and the two Sidneys . . . Those Americans are great but they are not sublime Man – the humanity of the United States can never reach the sublime.

But maybe an Englishman with poetry in his heart could beget a great American poet. That was the 'prophecy' John

Keats wrote for his brother George in 1819 upon learning that George and his wife were expecting their first child: perhaps their infant would grow up to be 'the first American poet', a writer who 'dares what no one dares':

> It lifts its little hand into the flame
> Unharm'd, and on the strings
> Paddles a little tune, and sings
> With dumb endeavour sweetly!
> Bard art thou completely,
> Little child
> O' the western wild,
> Bard art thou completely!
> Sweetly with dumb endeavour,
> A poet now or never . . .

Here is a poetic endeavour indeed: the western world would need to produce its own bard.

But many continued to doubt whether America could ever prove capable of such a feat, not least because (the argument went) they lacked the cultural and historical mettle to forge an as-yet-uncreated national literature. Throughout the nineteenth century, American writers were themselves often the first to concur.

Seven years after Keats died, in his 1828 travelogue 'Notions of the Americans', James Fenimore Cooper declared that aspiring American writers were crippled by a 'poverty of materials':

> There are no annals for the Historian; no follies (beyond the most vulgar and commonplace) for the satirist; no manners for the dramatist; no obscure fictions for the writer of romance; no gross and hourly offenses against decorum for the moralist; nor any of the rich artificial auxiliaries of Poetry.

Four decades later, the argument was still being made. John William DeForest introduced a new phrase into literary history when he mused in an 1868 essay about when it might be possible to produce 'the Great American Novel – the picture of the ordinary emotions and manners of American existence'.

Although a novel might prove possible, DeForest was certain 'that the Great American Poem will not be written, no matter what genius attempts it, until democracy, the idea of our day and nation and race, has agonized and conquered through centuries, and made its work secure'. This may have come as disappointing news to a poet named Walt Whitman, born in 1819, the same year that Keats presaged the birth of the first great American poet. Whitman had published *Leaves of Grass* a full thirteen years before DeForest's essay, but he doesn't even earn an honourable mention. Great American poetry was an endeavour for another day – but maybe Americans could scrape together sufficient art to produce something more prosaic in the meantime?

Afraid not, DeForest answered. Irving had been 'too cautious to make the trial', Cooper 'shirked the experiment', Hawthorne had written 'three delightful romances' but showed only 'a vague consciousness of this [American] life'. *Uncle Tom's Cabin* had come closest, but to anyone asking if the time had yet come for the Great American Novel, he answered: 'Wait.'

Another decade passed while America and the world waited, and then a young writer named Henry James sailed onto the American scene. In 1879, he produced his only extended work of literary criticism about someone else (James reserved most of his critical energies for his own novels, evidently judging that his contemporaries weren't up to the task). In *Hawthorne*, James made the same complaint that Cooper had made fifty years earlier, only more so, offering a famous catalogue of 'the items of high civilization' that were 'absent from the texture of American life':

> No State, in the European sense of the word, and indeed barely a specific national name. No sovereign, no court, no personal loyalty, no aristocracy, no church, no clergy, no army, no diplomatic service, no country gentlemen, no palaces, no castles, nor manors, nor old country-houses, nor parsonages, nor thatched cottages nor ivied ruins; no cathedrals, nor abbeys, nor little Norman churches; no great Universities nor public schools – no Oxford, nor Eton, nor Harrow; no literature, no novels, no museums, no pictures, no political society, no sporting class – no Epsom nor Ascot!

But these were the necessary wellsprings of the writer: 'it takes such an accumulation of history and custom, such a complexity of manners and types, to form a fund of suggestion for a novelist', James declared.

The endeavour to create a bard of the Western world had a long way to go.

1916

—

B Y the end of 1916, the idea that American art and culture were by definition second-rate had become a truism, a national inferiority complex. Could the New World ever produce an art worthy of the name, able to compete with the geniuses of the Old? Given that a list of the most memorable American novels published over the following year would begin with Edith Wharton's *Summer*, Sherwood Anderson's *Windy McPherson's Son* and two post-humous, unfinished novels by Henry James, it wouldn't have looked promising.

During those months, another impecunious, ambitious young writer was seeking inspiration from other writers – including Keats. In his final year at university, he drafted a poem that ends:

this midnight I aspire
To see, mirrored among the embers, curled,
In flame, the splendor and the sadness of the world.

He had been neglecting his classical studies, as he was the first to admit, also composing a parody of Keats's ode 'To A Grecian Urn', entitled 'To My Unused Greek Book (Acknowledgments to Keats)'. But he was avidly reading modern literature, informing a friend around this time: 'I want to be one of the greatest writers who ever lived, don't you?' The friend had not himself entertained this 'fantasy', he later reported, but although finding the remark 'rather foolish' at the time, he also couldn't help but respect his friend's eagerness. 'I am sure that his intoxicated ardour represented the healthy way for a young man of talent to feel,' Edmund Wilson, who would become a great critic himself, admitted later.

Part of the reason this endeavour seemed so foolish when it was blurted out around 1917 was that no American writer had ever yet been widely acknowledged as one of the greatest who ever lived. A year later, the influential critic Van Wyck Brooks was still writing of 'the desire, the aspiration, the struggle, the tentative endeavour' to create an American art worthy of the name, and of the need for a national 'spiritual history' that might enable such endeavours.

But in the meantime, the aspiring writer had drafted his first novel, and fallen in love with a Southern belle who then threw him over. He was convinced she'd rejected him because he was poor, because she lacked faith that his writing could support them both. But he was determined to confound everyone who doubted him, including her, and by 1919 he had finished his novel and had it accepted for publication.

The hero of the novel, which is loosely autobiographical, likes to quote Keats, at one point declaiming all of 'Ode to a Nightingale' to the bushes. He doesn't believe he'll be a great poet: 'I don't catch the subtle things like "silver-snarling trumpets",' he explains, alluding to another of Keats's poems, 'The Eve of St Agnes'. But he reads 'enormously' in modern literature, 'rather surprised by his discovery' of a few 'excellent American novels': *Vandover and the Brute*, *The Damnation of Theron Ware* and *Jennie Gerhardt*.

The first two are entirely forgotten today, while *Jennie Gerhardt* is remembered primarily as lesser Dreiser by people unlikely to agree there's such a thing as greater Dreiser. But at the time they passed for surprisingly good American novels, in the judgement of an ambitious young writer trying to find the realms of gold, to discover that peak in Darien.

The news of his first novel's publication (and his sale of a few magazine stories to Hollywood) was sufficient to give his fiancée, the one with second thoughts, a third thought: she would marry him after all. The novel, and the young couple, would take America by storm that year: *This Side of Paradise* became a national phenomenon, as did Scott and Zelda Fitzgerald.

Two years and three books later, probably around his September birthday in 1922, Fitzgerald decided that a successful young author like himself had better keep an eye on posterity, as well as on his accounts, and started what he called a 'Ledger'. He began the ledger with his tongue in his cheek, but at the same time a sense of an awareness of the eyes of future generations upon him. His career was already impressive, and he thought maybe he should jot down a few highlights, just in case.

Filling in earlier years, to give himself a kind of capsule autobiography, he offered a marginal précis of each year of his life to date. Of the year he turned twenty, between 1916 and 1917, when he had struggled to formulate his literary ambitions and discover his realms of gold, he wrote that it was a 'pregnant year of endeavor . . . the foundation of my literary life'.

Five years later, the endeavour had taken clearer form. He had published his second novel (whose protagonist owns 'a yellowed illegible autograph letter of Keats's'); turning his thoughts to the next, he decided to take his own ambitions more seriously.

In 1922 D.H. Lawrence published *Studies in Classic American Literature*, in which he dismissed American literature as 'the false dawn': 'the real American day hasn't begun yet', he announced. Many in American literary circles were still anxiously agreeing. That summer the literary editor of the New York *Tribune* pronounced that there were only two things left for a genuine artist in America to do – stay drunk or commit suicide.

But the centre of literary power was starting to show signs of shifting west, he also acknowledged. 'American literature, for the first time, it seems, is being treated with seriousness and respect by English critics. The recent reviews of the novels of Joseph Hergesheimer, Floyd Dell, Newton Fuessle, Scott Fitzgerald, Stephen Benét, Harry Leon Wilson and others are peppered with the adjectives of praise.'

At this precise moment, during the summer of 1922, Fitzgerald – whose work was making English critics sit up – began to think about writing the novel that would become *The Great Gatsby*. Not until July 1923 did he actually begin drafting the novel, amidst many parties. At one of them, Scott and Zelda ran into the same *Tribune* editor, who reported that Fitzgerald 'told us the plot of "the great American novel" which he is just writing (and asked me not to give it away)'. The editor's tone in reporting those ambitions was decidedly derisive; three months earlier, William Carlos Williams had just published an experimental, kaleidoscopic book reflecting on the impossibility of writing a great American novel, called *The Great American Novel*.

Certainly no one would have believed that Scott Fitzgerald of all people, a popular, talented but apparently wildly undisciplined novelist, would be the one to pull it off.

But here's one of many ironies in the story: if there's a single passage in *Gatsby* that does just that, it's the novel's famous closing elegiac account of the sailors who first viewed, with wild surmise, the grandeur of the Americas. The power of the novel comes from the way its jazz poetry about modern life builds to a moment of discovering the new world.

> For a transitory enchanted moment man must have held his breath in the presence of this continent, compelled into an aesthetic contemplation he neither understood nor desired, face to face for the last time in history with something commensurate to his capacity for wonder.

Looking with wild surmise, silent, upon a peak in Darien.

The Dutch merchants landing in New York, as Fitzgerald implies, were no less in search of realms of gold than the Spanish conquistadors who'd ventured further south. And that famous passage, in which Nick Carraway reflects on the meanings of America and its potential for aesthetic inspiration, was originally written at the end of the first chapter, not at the end of the novel. In other words, it is very possible that Fitzgerald had already drafted the passage that would go farther than any other to cement his claim to having written the great American novel when he told Long Island party-goers that summer that he was writing it.

That is not the only Keats in *Gatsby* – not by a long shot. Fitzgerald reworked lines and images, modernising the metaphors. He even smuggled in the silver snarling trumpets from Keats's 'Eve of St Agnes' ('probably the finest technical poem in English', he called it) – the precise phrase that his alter ego had worried five years earlier he'd always fumble.

Here they are not trumpets, but a jazzy transposition of Keats's celestial music: 'The moon had risen higher, and floating in the Sound was a triangle of silver scales, trembling a little to the stiff, tinny drip of the banjoes on the lawn.' These are the silver snarling trumpets for jazz-age Long Island, beyond the house 'glowing to receive a thousand guests', its host standing 'with heart on fire', just as in Keats's vision.

Like 'Chapman's Homer', Fitzgerald's first great novel is about endeavour, about ambition without a fixed purpose. But instead of exalted revelation, this is a tragedy, the tale of what happens when such ambition attaches itself to degraded goals. Jay Gatsby has all the things it takes to pursue a dream, the holy grail of his grand ambitions. But in this story tenacity becomes a tragic flaw, like hubris. He can't survive without his dreams – they define him, and his artistic capacities. But they also destroy him, because they were the wrong dreams.

In a line from *Gatsby*'s earliest surviving draft that he deleted from the novel, Fitzgerald described Gatsby as physically growing 'to be like the unsubstantiated idea that possessed him', which blurred him until he was unrecognisable, unreadable, illegible. Similarly, Fitzgerald wrote at the novel's very end that Gatsby 'believed in the green glimmer' – nothing so definite as the famous green light. Just a glimmer, a sense of something beyond one's ken.

The novel Fitzgerald produced is about the force of vision and will that is necessary to sustain any impossible project. If *The Great Gatsby* were merely concerned with the failure of Gatsby's vision, it would be only, as many critics have deemed it, an elegy for one imagined man. But because Fitzgerald links that vision with a high requiem for the nation, it becomes not Gatsby's doomed spiritual endeavour but

153

Fitzgerald's successful aesthetic one, in which he seizes the past, with the help of Keats, in order to redefine the present and conquer the future.

1926

IN April 1926, exactly a year after the publication of *The Great Gatsby*, another aspiring American writer published his first novel. A brief collection of portraits, loosely held together by overlapping characters, it might well be called a novella, or even sketches. The writer is not forgotten but his novel largely has been; it was called *The Cabala*, and it was written by Thornton Wilder, who would go on to much greater fame as the author of *The Bridge of San Luis Rey* and classic plays including *Our Town*.

Set in Rome after the First World War, it features a young American writer encountering high society in a city where the ancient gods still walk, but in modern decline. The shade of Virgil lingers, as does an unnamed young poet, promising but 'awfully adjectival', lying on his deathbed ('dead-poor') in seedy rooms next to the Spanish Steps.

The poet is bright-eyed with fever but wants to talk to his new American acquaintances, mentioning a brother who lives in New Jersey ('I was to have gone over there'). Visitors offer to read to him, perhaps an improvised translation of Homer. That is what he would like most of all, the poet cries: 'I know Chapman's well.'

The narrator responds, 'unthinking, that Chapman's was scarcely Homer at all, and suddenly beheld a look of pain, as of a mortal wound, appear on his face'. Horrified, the narrator 'hastened to add that in its way it was very beautiful, but I could not recall my cruelty; his heart seemed to have commenced bleeding within him'. They try to change the subject, 'but the insult to Chapman had been working in him', and the poet begins to weep.

To cheer him, the narrator launches into encomia for all the great writers, when suddenly the poet bursts out: 'I was meant to be among those names. I was . . . I was. I was. But now it's too late.' He declares he wants every copy of his books destroyed and asks them to make him a promise. 'There must be no name on my grave. Just write: Here lies one whose name was writ in water.'

1935

I N 1935, Fitzgerald's fourth novel had just been published, for which his ambitions had been high. It borrowed its title from Keats's 'Ode to a Nightingale': *Tender Is the Night*. Its themes, like the poem its title invoked, were the ancient ones of human mortality and the hope that the endeavour of art might provide a kind of immortality, while also asking whether art could produce beauty or truth. The novel even tips its hat directly to Keats, when Dick Diver goes to Rome and walks 'through the foul tunnel up to the Spanish Steps, where his spirit soared before the flower stalls and the house where Keats had died'.

When *Tender Is the Night* failed, so did Fitzgerald, spiralling into uncontrolled alcoholism and the year of what he would call 'the crack-up'.

As history happens, during that same terrible year a signed copy of *This Side of Paradise*, published fifteen years earlier, was auctioned off at someone else's profit, while Fitzgerald was trying to pull himself out of debt. It was the first time that any of his works had been sold at auction; he was so negligible a figure by this point that no one made a note of the amount it earned. He likely never even knew it had been sold.

Given the humiliations he endured that year, that's just as well; Fitzgerald would never have missed the symbolic implications of another writer junking his eager, charged claim to have discovered the realms of gold.

Four years later, Fitzgerald drew up a reading list, a 'curriculum' for his new lover, who had little formal education, and wanted to improve herself. But he was also almost certainly seeking a life-raft himself, as he tried to pull himself out of the dark waters of alcoholism, illness, failure and debt, and climb his way back into the wild surmise necessary to complete a fifth novel.

His curriculum included 'A Short Introduction to Poetry (with interruptions)', which opened with five poems by Keats: passages from 'The Eve of St Agnes' and 'The Pot of Basil', 'Bright Star' and 'When I Have Fears', another poem about fame and immortality:

> When I have fears that I may cease to be . . .
> then on the shore
> Of the wide world I stand alone, and think
> Till love and fame to nothingness do sink.

The fifth Keats poem on the curriculum was 'On First Looking into Chapman's Homer'.

Next to Chapman's Homer, Fitzgerald jotted a marginal note: 'Re-read Wilder'. Under the American short story, he listed Henry James, Ring Lardner, Gertrude Stein and 'The Cabala, Wilde'. It's a typo for Wilder: he would always be drawn to jazz-age renderings of Keats.

On September 25, 1940 – the day after his forty-fourth birthday – Fitzgerald returned to a friend a volume he had borrowed, with a note of thanks: 'I am sending you the Chapman to your house with postage . . . I had read Lang,

Leaf and Myers' *Iliad* and Butler's *Odyssey* and most of Pope's dribble but for years have wanted to read Chapman – probably on account of Keats's sonnet. Now I have, thanks to you and feel greatly improved and highly Elizabethan.'

Three months later, he was dead. His epitaph did not declare his name was written on water but it invoked water all the same: 'So we beat on, boats against the current, borne back ceaselessly into the past.' The endeavour is circular: our voyages of discovery always take us back into the past.

A few months before his death, Fitzgerald wrote to his daughter, advising her to read Keats. 'Poetry is either something that lives like fire inside you,' he explained, 'or else it is nothing . . . The Grecian Urn is unbearably beautiful with every syllable as inevitable as the notes in Beethoven's Ninth Symphony or it's just something you don't understand. It is what it is because an extraordinary genius paused at that point in history and touched it.' Once you'd come to understand it, to know what men might mean by it, why then 'one could scarcely ever afterwards be unable to distinguish between gold and dross in what one read'.

Afterwards one would choose only to travel in realms of gold, in search of peaks in Darien.

CONTRIBUTORS

ELEY WILLIAMS is a writer and lecturer based in Ealing. Her collection of short stories, *Attrib. And Other Stories* (Influx Press), was chosen by Ali Smith as one of the best debut works of fiction published in 2017. Twice shortlisted for the *White Review* Short Story Prize, her work has appeared in the *London Review of Books*, the *White Review*, *Ambit* and the *Cambridge Literary Review*. She has a pamphlet of poetry titled *Frit* (Sad Press), and is currently co-editor of fiction at online journal *3:AM Magazine*.

DAVID SZALAY is the author of five works of fiction: *Spring*, *The Innocent*, *London and the South-East*, for which he was awarded the Betty Trask and Geoffrey Faber Memorial Prizes, *All That Man Is*, for which he was awarded the Gordon Burn Prize and Plimpton Prize for Fiction, and shortlisted for the Man Booker Prize, and *Turbulence*. Born in Canada, he grew up in London, and now lives in Budapest.

KAMILA SHAMSIE wrote her first novel, *In The City by the Sea*, while still in college, and it was published in 1998 when she was twenty-five. It was shortlisted for the John Llewellyn Rhys Prize in the UK, and Shamsie received the Prime Minister's Award for Literature in Pakistan in 1999. Her second novel, *Salt and Saffron*, followed in 2000, after which she was selected as one of Orange's Twenty-One Writers of the twenty-first century. Her fifth novel, *Burnt Shadows* (2009), was shortlisted for the Orange Prize for Fiction and won an Anisfield-Wolf Book Award for fiction. Her seventh novel, *Home Fire*, was longlisted for the 2017 Booker Prize, and in 2018 won the Women's Prize for Fiction. In 2013 she was included in the Granta list of twenty best young British writers. She is a Fellow of the Royal Society of Literature.

MAX PORTER's first novel, *Grief Is the Thing with Feathers*, won the *Sunday Times*/Peter, Fraser + Dunlop Young Writer of the Year, the International Dylan Thomas Prize, the Europese Literatuurprijs and the BAMB Readers' Award and was shortlisted for the *Guardian* First Book Award and the Goldsmiths Prize. It has been sold in twenty-nine territories. His second novel, *Lanny*, was published in March 2019. Complicité and Wayward's production of *Grief Is the Thing with Feathers*, directed by Enda Walsh and starring Cillian Murphy, opened in Dublin in March 2018 and transferred to the Barbican in London in March 2019.

SARA COLLINS is of Jamaican descent and grew up in Grand Cayman. She studied law at the London School of Economics and worked as a lawyer for seventeen years before doing a Master of Studies in Creative Writing at Cambridge University, where she was the recipient of the 2015 Michael Holroyd Prize for Creative Writing. Her first novel, *The Confessions of Frannie Langton*, was published to widespread acclaim in 2019.

DAISY JOHNSON was born in 1990 and is a British novelist and short story writer. In 2017, she published the short story collection *Fen*. Her debut novel, *Everything Under*, was short-listed for the 2018 Booker Prize, and she is the youngest nominee in the prize's history. For her short stories, she has won three awards since 2014.

TASH AW was born in Taipei to Malaysian parents. He grew up in Kuala Lumpur before moving to Britain to attend university. He is the author of four critically acclaimed novels – *The Harmony Silk Factory* (2005), which won the

Whitbread First Novel Award and a regional Commonwealth Writers' Prize; *Map of the Invisible World* (2009); *Five Star Billionaire* (2013) and *We, The Survivors* (2019) – and a work of non-fiction, *The Face: Strangers on a Pier* (2016), finalist for the *LA Times* Book Prize. His novels have twice been longlisted for the Man Booker Prize and been translated into twenty-three languages. His work has won an O. Henry Prize and been published in the *New Yorker*, the *London Review of Books*, *A Public Space* and the landmark *Granta 100*, amongst others. He is also a contributing opinion writer for the *New York Times*.

PETER FRANKOPAN is Professor of Global History at Oxford University, where he is also Senior Research Fellow at Worcester College, Oxford, and Director of the Oxford Centre for Byzantine Research. His book *Silk Roads* went to number one in the *Sunday Times* Non-Fiction charts, remaining in the Top Ten for nine months in a row, as well as being number one in China, India and many other countries around the world. His follow-up, *The New Silk Roads*, is a 'masterly mapping out of a new world order', according to the *Evening Standard*. In December 2018, *The Silk Roads* was chosen as one of the twenty-five most influential books translated into Chinese in the last forty years.

YAN GE was born in 1984 in Sichuan, and currently lives in Dublin. She recently completed a PhD in Comparative Literature at Sichuan University and is the chairperson of the China Young Writers Association. *People's Literature* magazine recently chose her – in a list reminiscent of the *New Yorker*'s 'Twenty under forty' – as one of China's twenty future literary masters, and in 2012 she was chosen as Best New Writer by the prestigious Chinese Literature Media Prize. Yan Ge was a guest writer at the Netherlands Crossing Borders Festival in The Hague, November 2012, and since then has appeared at numerous literary festivals in Europe. Her novel *The Chilli Bean Paste Clan* was published in Chinese in May 2013 by Zhejiang Literature Press, and has been translated into German, French and several other languages.

LAWRENCE OSBORNE is the author of the critically acclaimed novels *The Forgiven, The Ballad of a Small Player, Hunters in the Dark, Beautiful Animals,* and six books of non-fiction. He is the third writer, after John Banville (writing as Benjamin Black) and Robert B. Parker, to be asked by the Raymond Chandler Estate to write a new Philip Marlowe novel. Osborne lives in Bangkok.

KATHARINE KILALEA grew up in South Africa and moved to the UK to study for an M.A. in Creative Writing at the University of East Anglia. Her debut poetry collection, *One Eye'd Leigh* (2009), was shortlisted for the Costa Poetry Award and longlisted for the Dylan Thomas Prize. Katharine's debut novel, *OK, Mr Field,* was published in early June 2018 by Faber & Faber, and in the US in early July 2018 by Tim Duggan Books.

MICHAEL DONKOR was born in London in 1985. He was raised in a Ghanaian household where talking lots and reading lots were vigorously encouraged. Michael worked in publishing for a number of years, but eventually decided to put his literary enthusiasms to other uses: in 2010, he retrained as an English teacher. Since then he has taught A-Level English, trying to develop a curious excitement about books and storytelling within his students. In 2014 Michael was selected by Writers Centre Norwich for their Inspires Mentoring Scheme, and worked with mentor Daniel Hahn. His first novel, *Hold,* which explores Ghanaian heritage and questions surrounding sexuality, identity and sacrifice, was published by 4th Estate in July 2018.

BENJAMIN MARKOVITS grew up in Texas, London, Oxford and Berlin. He left an unpromising career as a professional basketball player to study the Romantics – an experience he wrote about in *Playing Days*, a novel. He has published seven novels, including *Either Side of Winter*, about a New York private school, and a trilogy on the life of Lord Byron: *Imposture*, *A Quiet Adjustment* and *Childish Loves*. *Granta* selected him as one of the Best of Young British Novelists in 2013. In 2016, his novel *You Don't Have To Live Like This* was awarded the James Tait Black Prize for Fiction.

ALEX PRESTON is an award-winning novelist and journalist. He is the author of three novels, most recently the critically acclaimed *In Love and War*, as well as a bestselling literary history of birds, *As Kingfishers Catch Fire*. His short stories have appeared several times in the *Best British Short Stories* anthology. He writes regularly for the *Observer*, the *Telegraph* and *Harper's Bazaar*.

SARAH CHURCHWELL is Professorial Fellow in American Literature and Chair of Public Understanding of the Humanities at the School of Advanced Study, University of London. Her books include *The Many Lives of Marilyn Monroe* (2004), *Careless People: Murder, Mayhem and the Invention of The Great Gatsby* (2013) and *Behold America – A History of America First and the American Dream*. Churchwell appears regularly on television and radio and is the director of the Being Human Festival.